For A, my real life hero

Diversion Books
A Division of Diversion Publishing Corp.
443 Park Avenue South, Suite 1008
New York, New York 10016
www.DiversionBooks.com

For more information, email info@diversionbooks.com

First Diversion Books edition June 2014.

Print ISBN: 978-1-62681-354-0
eBook ISBN: 978-1-62681-310-6

The Job Proposal

WENDY CHEN

DIVERSIONBOOKS

Chapter 1

Kate stayed perfectly still in her bed until she heard the telltale sound of the front door closing tightly behind her latest overnight guest before emerging from under her covers.

There was little better in life than being able to belt out your favorite song in the middle of a hot shower—especially after a particularly *satisfying* evening. She especially loved singing "Seasons of Love" from *RENT* because it reminded her of her high school glee club days in Michigan, when she only *dreamt* about living in New York City.

Big city life on the East Coast had always held appeal. But High School Kate, whose only friend was a fellow math team nerd, could never have imagined the casual dating lifestyle would suit her so well. She shuddered at the prospect of ever having to endure the kind of romantic angst she'd seen her friends go through. She remembered precisely when it happened, when she had that epiphanal moment that set her on a course toward romantic freedom. During their junior year at Columbia, one of her friends had sat on the couch, which had seen too many beer stains and who knows what else, bawling into a hand towel because they'd run out of tissues. "He didn't caaaaalllll," she'd wailed. "We had s-s-s-s-uch a g-g-g—ood tiiiiime." She'd gone on to worse after that, even after she'd calmed down. "I feel so cheap," she'd said. And just like that, Kate swore that no man would ever have that kind of power over her.

There was freedom in being able to enjoy the company of men on their own terms, Kate found. There was no pressure to impress, but all the reason to flirt and just have *fun*. The key, Kate found, was not to *lower* expectations, per se, but to keep her expectations to where they mattered most—in the bedroom. And indeed, she had high expectations in that realm. Last night's companion fulfilled them nicely, and now she could get on with her day without checking her phone every five minutes to see if he'd texted.

"You've got quite a voice there." Kate jolted her eyes open and stood up straighter, trying not to show too much surprise and annoyance at the intrusion. If she had wanted company, she certainly would not have feigned sleep during the entire time he was leaving a note on her bedside table. It was kind of sweet that he would write a note to say good-bye, and it was certainly more than she expected. Of course, if she'd thought the note mattered, she might have read it. "What song is that?" he asked.

Oh my God. She knew he was young, but she didn't know he lived under a rock. "An old Broadway show tune." She turned off the shower. "Hand me that towel, will you?" He obliged and turned his gaze away from her. Kate smiled. It was cute that he was embarrassed. There was a time in her life when she would have been embarrassed, too. "Don't feel like you need to stick around," she said, not unkindly. "You don't need to worry about my morning after."

"I got us breakfast!" he said excitedly. "I left you a note so you wouldn't think I'd just left." Kate followed him out to her little dining table, still wearing only a towel. "I got muffins, some oatmeal—I wasn't sure what you'd want. Cappuccino and mocha and just straight-up coffee, too."

"This is so unexpected." He gave her a shy smile that made her think if she were a different kind of girl, she'd be grinning back at him, thinking this attraction was going somewhere. She picked at a muffin and sipped at the cap so his feelings didn't get hurt.

"You're sweet," she said and meant it. He was sweet last night at the bar, too, catching her eye while he played guitar and sang cover songs. On his break, he sent over a drink and a cheesy poem written on a napkin—song*writer* he clearly was not.

A few years ago, she might have skipped the sex and anxiously awaited a phone call, to be asked to dinner, for flowers to be delivered at the office if the date went well. But she knew his type: the charmer who liked the thrill of the chase.

It always began with the usual optimistic anticipation—*Will he call? He seemed interested, didn't he?* And the heady excitement that came with new attraction and romance. Then, right around the ninety-day mark, things would start to go awry, with that awkward "are we exclusive" conversation. (The more awkward the conversation, the louder the warning bells!) The next stage was around six months, when future vacations or holidays would need to be planned. Lots of guys made exits around then. Kate quickly learned it was a lot more fun to take a rule from their playbook and always keep the relationship fresh and new rather than deal with the inevitable discovery that it wasn't true love.

"I've got to get in to work today, though, so I don't want to keep you …"

"Work? It's Sunday."

"I'm working on a big deal—"

"OK, OK, I'll just have breakfast while you get dressed. I'll walk you to work."

The poor kid. Maybe he really was a good guy. That meant he was going to get his heart broken badly one day if he hadn't already. She covered his hand with hers.

"Listen, Jake. The thing is, my fiancé will be getting home soon." She was surprised at how easily the words rolled off her tongue. The end justified the means.

Jake bolted up from his chair as if someone had appeared with a shotgun aimed right at him. "Your *fiancé*? You have a fiancé?"

She swallowed the guilt she felt at seeing Jake's stricken face. It was really better this way, better than trying to explain that he would come to regret getting mixed up with her. She was bound to disappoint him somewhere down the line, and it was better to send him off now, with the fresh memory of a great night together. And now he'd have a good story for his buddies—how he'd slept with an almost-married woman.

"Hey, hey, don't freak out! It's not like *that*," Kate said, feigning defensiveness. "We have an open relationship. We just don't rub it in each other's face, that's all. Common courtesy."

Jake looked at her like she was some kind of crazy. But at least that was better than looking like he wanted to date her. This wasn't supposed to be this awkward. She'd pegged him as the "that was great, I'll see you around" mumbling type who headed for the door as quickly as he could. The first time that happened, she'd sat in her bed alone for hours, not quite knowing what to do. Then she'd come to realize that life was much simpler when you maintained control over your emotions and knew what to expect—and Jake would come to realize that, too.

No strings, no drama, no broken hearts.

After Jake left, Kate texted her girls.

This engagement thing really comes in handy.

It had been about two months since she announced her engagement. At first, she thought she was just helping out a friend, telling him that she would marry him if his green card didn't work out and his visa expired at the end of the year.

But Kate was starting to enjoy being engaged. She'd found it tiresome to hear her coworkers' same old comments about what they thought her life was like.

"New year, new guy?" was popular during holiday parties.

"A free-spirited, single girl like you just wouldn't understand trying to balance work and family" was the more common theme. Kate literally bit her tongue when her boss said to her, all too regularly, some variation of "Mondays must be hard for you after a weekend of partying."

With an idiot boss who often made business decisions based on personal impressions, Kate needed to adjust her reputation at work. She couldn't control what was said, but she could offer less ammunition for anyone to question her dedication to her work. Even though she'd made vice president by working her tail off during her early days at the firm, as a thirty-five-year-old woman who was ten years out of B-school, she felt like she needed to present herself as someone more stable, someone who could handle more responsibility. Once she told her colleagues about her betrothal, she swore her reputation at the firm immediately went up a couple of notches.

The problem was the next step. Several of her peers from B-school were *senior* vice presidents now, at least the men and women who didn't take a baby break. And when her mother sent her an *Elle* magazine article about movers and shakers under age forty, there was no personal note to accompany it. But Kate could take the hint nonetheless.

In her view, Kate was doing a small favor for Alberto and using a little white lie to give her professional reputation a boost. The added benefit of a fiancé to scare off would-be suitors was just a bonus.

Kate yawned. It was 8 a.m. already. She really had slept in. She hurried to pull on her running tank and shorts and adjusted her socks and sneakers while she waited for the elevator. The look on Jake's face as he rushed out of her apartment was assurance that he had hightailed it back to his Queens walk-up and there would be no risk of bumping into him. She felt bad enough already; there was no reason to rub it in that she was actively avoiding him.

Kate loved her neighborhood, so much more than the uptown dorms of Columbia, where she had gotten her undergraduate degree. She had lived on the Lower West Side of Manhattan ever since she went to NYU for grad school. And today, like almost every other day, she headed straight toward the waterfront for her morning jog. Sometimes Kate still couldn't quite believe she lived in New York City, that she lived *successfully and comfortably*, actually, a life she had only seen in the movies while growing up. Oh yes, Kate thought as she turned to look at the towering skyline, from scrawny Katie Wallace to Kate on Wall Street, this girl from Michigan was doing pretty well for herself.

After a few miles, Kate headed home for her shower, running into the hot blond who lived a few floors below her. He seemed just her type—good-looking, tall, athletic build—but she only gave him a cursory hello as he was leaving. Kate had few rules about men, and she meant to keep them. "Rule

Number One," Kate sighed to the empty elevator. "Never sleep with your neighbor." It could get too complicated too quickly.

By 10 a.m., Kate was in her office, dressed in a pencil skirt and tank blouse. Her hair was down, the only nod to a more casual appearance than she would normally have during the week. She was the only one in the office, as was common for a Sunday when her colleagues were spending time with their families or recovering from partying. She would spend a few hours here, getting organized for the week ahead. Senior VP titles weren't given to people who were lazy.

Chapter 2

It had been weeks since Kate posted a change in her relationship status on Facebook. Four weeks and two days, in fact, since Adam saw that stupid little red heart pop up next to her name on his news feed. He had pinged her then, a private message to stand out from the clutter on her wall from other incredulous friends. Like all the others, he wanted to know if this was for real. But unlike the others, who seemed to just find amusement at Kate's ability to fall in love—or at least lust—all the time, Adam knew that once she fell for real, she would fall fast and hard. Could this be it and he missed it?

He looked at his message to her and sighed.

Engaged? For real?

He had wanted to keep his inquiry casual, nothing to betray the sense of—what?—the sense of loss that he felt when he saw her status change? Loss wasn't the word. He missed her, he supposed. Or maybe he just missed knowing that she was single, that she was always single, even when he was in relationships himself.

There was still no reply from her, so Adam poked around her profile page, scrolling through the various postings. It looked like she hadn't been on Facebook since she posted that damned relationship update, so he didn't feel quite so bad. He looked through her photos, including one that someone else had posted of her in high school, a group shot of the glee club she had been in. He was a bit surprised that she hadn't untagged herself—she just looked so different now. She was his best friend in high school—his only friend, really—and it never occurred to him that the waist-length braid she wore every day or the baggy clothes she wore over her skinny frame were anything but normal. She was just *Katie*. But then he looked at a recent photo of her at some party, with her strawberry blond hair hanging in waves, wearing a strapless mini dress. She still had the same megawatt smile, one that didn't show itself all that often in high school, particularly when she complained that her mouth and teeth were too big. Her eyes were the same, too—hazel with sparkle when she laughed. He imagined they still gave away nothing about her emotions and her thoughts when she chose not to. Adam toggled between the two pictures and swallowed the lump that had suddenly formed in his throat. He honestly wasn't sure which photo he liked best.

He sometimes still felt badly about how they lost touch. He had assumed that after high school they would just drift apart like friends often do, especially since he would be at Stanford and she at Columbia. How much farther apart could they have gone? He hadn't expected to hear from her quite so often that first fall semester. His roommate kept asking if Kate was his girlfriend, as if he had ever thought of their relationship as anything but platonic. Once, when Adam actually did have a girl he liked in his dorm room, he practically hung up on Kate when she called. But even that hadn't been enough to brush her off. She announced that she was going to come visit him for a weekend since she had found a cheap last-minute airfare.

Adam had gotten so annoyed with Kate that weekend, how she wouldn't stop trailing him like a lost puppy. He was finally, *finally* finding a group of friends that he had things in common with, ones who actually thought it was cool that he'd built a computer himself and were envious that he'd been able to skip the introductory Computer Science class that other freshmen took. He'd dragged Kate to a party, partly to avoid having to just *talk* to her, and partly because he thought they'd have fun. But she sat in a corner nursing a plastic cup of beer until he felt badly enough to leave early with her.

On the walk back to his dorm, he'd been a little drunk

and more than a little annoyed, and they had finally had it out. *What's your problem?* he had said to her. *You have to stop needing me so much. Stop calling me all the time. Get your own life.* He couldn't really remember her reaction or what she'd said, only that she hadn't cried, thank goodness. She had been pretty quiet and had just continued to walk next to him back to his dorm. The next morning they acted like nothing had happened while he drove her to the airport and made idle chitchat about plans for Thanksgiving.

She didn't call him after that visit, not even during holiday breaks when they were both back in Michigan. He didn't see her again until after junior year, when they ran into each other in Ann Arbor during the summer. He almost hadn't recognized her when she'd called out his name at the mall. It wasn't just that she had cut her hair, it was that her entire demeanor had been different—she had been almost exuberant as she chattered excitedly about how great it was to see him and how he should come out to a club near the university, where she was meeting up with some friends that night.

Kate's friends turned out to be some U of M students that she'd met during her temp job at the university, but he never would have guessed that she had just met them a week ago by how they laughed at her stories, by how she confidently ordered rounds of drinks, by how she barely stepped off the dance floor. He still recognized the old Katie when she spoke to him and when she sang along to the music, but this girl had *sparkled*.

Adam had returned to Palo Alto soon after that night, to go back to his internship at Apple. They barely saw each other in person again, except during the odd holiday when they both happened to be visiting their parents. Those visits became less and less frequent for both of them as they spent more time on their respective coasts building their careers. Now their friendship mostly consisted of the occasional Facebook post or email.

Adam sighed. He wondered if it was time for him to leave the Bay Area. He had gone from undergrad to grad school, from one tech start-up to another for the past fifteen years. He'd worked his tail off—and had been lucky—almost every time. He had loved it for a long time. But maybe it was time to do something new, something that was about more than the business pitch and making money. And if he was being truthful with himself, he wouldn't mind a little distance from Claudia, his fiancée … *ex*-fiancée … who made him feel a sense of overwhelming guilt every time he saw her, or their house, or any one of their mutual friends. And after being together for the past five years, pretty much all his friends were mutual friends.

Chapter 3

Sunday evenings were often spent with the girls—Cassandra, Suzanne, Mia, and Kate. Kate had met all three when they were at NYU, she in business school while the others were undergrads in a Finance class that she was a teaching assistant for. It wasn't all that common for a graduate student to hang out with undergrads, and the four always had very different personalities, but somehow they complemented and balanced one another.

Tonight they were trying out a new restaurant in Chelsea, so Kate decided to go with something fun that she knew the girls would get a kick out of—a pink wig. A cute, pale pink chin-length bob, to be exact, which went perfectly with her silver smoky eye makeup for a look that was edgy and slightly sweet. She threw on a silver strapless dress and a favorite pair of Jimmy Choos. Maybe she was a little overdressed, with jeans and flip-flops viewed as acceptable attire for nearly any occasion these days, but Kate *loved* getting dressed up. It wasn't until she was in college that she paid the least bit of attention to fashion, much less to cultivating her own sense of style. But once she started, she relished any opportunity to try out different looks, particularly ones that she couldn't get away with in the office. Kate put her phone, wallet, and keys into her tiny clutch, grabbed her "engagement ring" and headed out. She didn't always wear the ring—only her girls, Alberto, and Kate knew the true nature of the arrangement, and nothing was a bigger turnoff to men than a giant rock that looked real. But the girls were more than a little concerned about her decision, and she had to show them she was comfortable with her plans.

•   •   •

When Kate arrived at the restaurant, Cass noticed her first and did a double take before grinning widely at the new look. As usual, Kate was the last to arrive, but they'd already ordered her a dirty martini, and they did a quick toast to surviving the end of another workweek. Some friends would gather on a Friday night for this, but as a busy wedding planner, Cassandra rarely had weekends free. All three gushed for a moment about how much they loved Kate's wig, and Suzanne of course commented that only Kate could pull something like that off. But it was only a matter of minutes before they were peppering her with questions about Alberto again.

It seemed that it was Cass who was nominated to broach the topic this time, and Kate admitted that it made sense for her to ask what kind of celebration she planned on, and if Cass should pencil in a date to start the planning?

"Oh, nothing you have to worry about too much. I'm thinking we'll just go to Disney World and do the Cinderella castle thing," Kate said. She saw her friends' mouths agape and added, "I'm kidding, you guys. You know that's nothing like me."

"Getting *married* is nothing like you. Multiple dates with the same guy is nothing like you," said Mia, always the straight shooter of the bunch.

"Alberto is too talented a musician and loves New York too much to go back to Spain."

"And you're too fond of him as a bedmate." Mia and Cass clinked glasses in agreement.

"I have always been fond of friends with benefits," Kate laughed. She and Alberto had hit it off ever since the first week of business school, even when she took the straight and narrow path toward a career in investment management, while he developed buyer's remorse soon after graduation and gave up an offer at Lehman Brothers to become a starving artist. Kate supported him then—the fact that Lehman went bankrupt always served as evidence that he'd made the right decision—and she would now, as his back-up plan if he needed her.

"Marriage is really serious business," Suzanne chimed in. "Are you sure you're thinking this through?"

Kate wanted to keep this light, even though it was clear her friends had another agenda. "You of all people should be loving this, Suzanne! This is the old-fashioned arranged marriage between two friends. We'll have a prenup, of course. It's a business arrangement that happens to extend to the bedroom on occasion."

"But what if one of you wants more out of the relationship than that?" Suzanne asked, ever the romantic.

"Or what if one of you wants to get out of it?" Mia said matter-of-factly. "You could fall in love with someone else." Kate just stared at her. "OK, maybe *he* could fall in love with someone else."

"People get divorced *all the time*," Kate responded. She knew Suzanne recently found out that her ex-husband was getting remarried, and that Suzanne had not been having great luck with dating recently, so she wished they would move on from this topic. Her *arrangement* should not be, would not be the reason to dredge up heartbreak for her friend. "Anyway, we'll probably just do some City Hall ceremony once we find out for sure about his visa. I'll try to let you know ahead of time if you feel like coming." She could tell these responses were not satisfying her friends. "Listen," she said more seriously, "we all know that married people get all the perks—better job opportunities, better apartments, the list goes on. I've merely figured out how to reap the rewards without the baggage."

"Baggage like monogamy?" Suzanne said sarcastically.

"Exactly!" Kate responded brightly. "Now can we be done with this conversation?" She smiled at a guy at a table a few feet from theirs. But apparently he was on a date from the glare he got from his companion. Kate rolled her eyes. She wasn't a homewrecker, but believed in Rule Number Two: He's not "taken" unless he's *married*. The game's not over until the ring's on his finger.

"Speaking of monogamy," Kate said under her breath as she recognized a couple at a table several feet away. She gave a friendly wave and smiled. The man lifted his hand politely in response and the woman gave her a tight smile before they both turned away.

"You feel those daggers?" Cass rolled her eyes. "What did you do, sleep with her husband?"

Kate remembered being shocked at the news, the awkwardness in his voice when she'd called him to see if he wanted to get a drink a few nights after they'd slept together. How for a few weeks afterward she'd had to remind herself that she'd had as much fun as he did and that she'd gone into the hookup with no expectations. She shook off the memory and shrugged. "I had a crush on him in college. When we ran into each other a few years later, he said he was on a break from his girlfriend. Next thing I know, he's married." Kate grinned broadly, even though she didn't quite feel it. "This is why I can only be friends with you three. I can keep track of your men and avoid pissing off the entire female population of Manhattan." She took a big gulp of her drink. "Some people need to get out of the past."

Sometimes New York felt really, really small.

The rest of the evening felt a little more normal to Kate. They had more drinks, critiqued their food, and ate off each other's plates to make sure they all got to try a little of everything. She loved having girlfriends, knowing they cared about her enough to question her recent decisions. The fact that Cassandra and Mia were both in monogamous relationships and that Suzanne was always on the quest for the same made little difference. Kate knew that she was unlike most women in terms of how she actively avoided looking for Mr. Right and wasn't looking forward to starting a family—at all. The fact was, she had enough of a "family." She had these girls at this table, she had Alberto, she even had Adam when she felt nostalgic. They all fit in with her life in different ways. She just didn't need the traditional husband/wife/kids structure to feel fulfilled, and she certainly didn't need the kind of distractions to her career that a traditional family would create.

Back at home, Kate kicked off her shoes, shook her hair out of the wig, and pulled it back into a loose braid. She stayed in her dress as she sat at her computer, having paid enough for it that she didn't want to take it off right away. She looked at the pile of bills stacked neatly on her desk and decided to get them out of the way. She had learned from her mother all right and paid her credit card balances, always in full, always on time, even back when she had student loans to pay, even when she'd splurged a little that month. And just like every other month when she went through this routine of checking bank statements, receipts, and invoices, she was grateful that she'd followed her mother's advice *not* to follow in her footsteps. Kate didn't have to debate which bill would be paid late or not at all, didn't have to ask her spouse why he spent three hundred dollars at the bookstore.

She decided to check Facebook before going to bed. She didn't often post updates about herself and was certainly not one to share photos of her weekly mani/pedi like some. She hadn't initially thought of herself as a social network type of person, but its snapshot view of all her friends and family was addictive in a voyeuristic way. She had spent hours flipping through photos of old college friends, amazed at how their lives had changed since she'd first met them, wondered at the self-proclaimed cultural snob's choice of reading online celebrity gossip sites, and chuckled at how much time some colleagues spent playing games. And of course there was a part of her that just liked knowing more about their lives than they knew about hers.

She had a message from Adam, asking about her engagement like so many others had. She knew that updating her relationship status would generate some questions, but she didn't anticipate how many. Just because she didn't post "couple" photos and update her status in first person plural all the time, was it really so surprising that she could be in a relationship?

Well … maybe it was.

Thank goodness she had already told her parents, or at least her mother, before then. Linda Wallace would not have been pleased to find out about her only child's impending nuptials through a Facebook post. Linda—and Kate called her Linda—had taken the news about Kate marrying an old friend from business school just as Kate thought she would. She was skeptical about relationships in general, having divorced Kate's father after nearly twenty years of marriage. But as long as Kate kept her career and financial independence (and didn't mention Alberto was a *musician*), Linda wished her the best and would fly out for the wedding. And if there was anything else Kate wanted Linda to do, like those mother-of-the-bride type things that some of Linda's friends talked about, Kate should just let her know. There were no happy tears from Linda or emailed suggestions for wedding gowns or floral arrangements. The day after Kate told her, Linda had sent her a text:

If you buy an apartment make sure your name's on the title.

Followed by:

Nothing wrong with separate bank accounts for percentage of own earnings.

Kate wasn't sure what she wanted to tell Adam about the nature of her engagement. They'd become best friends after their freshman biology teacher sat them alphabetically, and Adam Ward was seated behind Katie Wallace. He'd borrowed a pen from her the first day of class, muttering something about his brothers melting the points on his, and he'd spent the rest of the semester whispering science jokes that only two geeks like them would find funny. There had been a time back in high school when she would have confided everything to him, when he had been her closest friend, helping her through her parents' divorce just by being around for her when she didn't want to be alone. She tried not to think about that time now; she had come so far from being that mousy, lonely girl. Adam had been vague about how his own relationship had ended several months ago, and she wasn't sure who he still kept in touch with from their hometown. Ultimately Kate didn't want to risk having to explain to Linda that the engagement was a business arrangement, so she only wrote back the standard answer she had been giving to everyone:

He's a guy from grad school. No date set yet.

A message from her father came in, and Kate groaned before she opened it. Dad was in pitch mode, and he had just sent out fifty letters to literary agents with his latest book proposal for a novel yet to be completed. Growing up, Kate's mother used to say what a brilliant writer her dad was, only he lacked focus. Kate didn't quite know what that meant back then, but she surely saw it now. Her dad had new ideas for his "next great novel" all the time and did not seem to be deterred by the fact that he had yet to complete the first one, the one that he'd been working on when he married her mother, the one that was going to take care of them all "as soon as he got an agent, as soon as he got a book deal." Thank goodness Dad had discovered blogging in the last few years and now had an outlet for all his snippets of ideas and opinions. When she was younger, he would proudly proclaim how much Kate was like him—how creative they both were, how much they enjoyed life. *As long as someone's supporting that life you enjoy,* Linda would mutter. "Good luck" was all Kate wrote back to him. What could she say? "Hope you don't get more rejections?" "How about finishing the first one?"

Kate went back to read a long message from her friend Elizabeth, her darling, darling friend Elizabeth, who had been her roommate at Columbia and whom she missed dearly ever since Elizabeth moved to the Midwest after college. She hadn't had time to read the message when it first came in and wanted to give it the attention it deserved. Elizabeth had married her college sweetheart and followed him to Chicago when he went to medical school before settling down in Minneapolis near his family. They had three kids now, and Elizabeth became a stay-at-home mom after their son developed some health issues. Kate knew parenthood sometimes wore her out more than she liked to admit. In this message, Elizabeth was saying how exhausted she was, having been up all night managing one kid's latest bout with asthma, another's sleep training, about how critical her mother-in-law has been, how disinterested her own parents have become, as retired Upper East Siders living in Palm Beach. Elizabeth's was not a life that Kate knew how to relate to, but she always felt she owed Elizabeth so much, that she truly loved her as if they had been sisters, that she tried hard to at least be the safe shoulder for Elizabeth to cry on.

When Kate met Elizabeth on that first day when everyone was moving into their dorms, she had felt intimidated by this outgoing girl who had already decorated her half of the room with Picasso and Monet posters and a garland of artificial flowers along the ceiling, and lined up ten pairs of shoes in all different styles. Kate had expected Elizabeth to take one look at the two (just two) suitcases that Kate had been able to bring on the plane and go ask for a room change. But instead Elizabeth sat cross-legged on her Calvin Klein comforter and chatted while Kate unpacked.

"It was smart not to bring too much with you. That way you can just buy what you need once you figure it out." Elizabeth snapped her gum in her teeth the way Kate had repeatedly tried … and failed. "I had to bring everything. It was either that or throw it out so my parents could have a guest room." She blew a bubble, then popped it. "I've never seen my dad as excited as he was pulling a U-Haul up to our building. They couldn't wait to get me out of the house," Elizabeth had said, chuckling. "Some people just should never be parents, you know?" Kate had just smiled, not wanting her new roommate to think she was passing judgment so quickly. But she'd felt the tension leave her shoulders then, with the knowledge that they had more in common than she'd initially thought.

When Kate self-consciously unpacked the meager two pairs of shoes she had brought, she first thought Elizabeth was making fun of her when she gushed over how cute the flowered sandals were. But she would soon learn that there wasn't anything disingenuous about Elizabeth. By the end of their first week of school, Kate realized that she had never met anyone quite like Elizabeth, a girl who had grown up with lots of financial privileges in New York, who had clearly never lacked for friends or popularity, who always seemed to have the right outfit and attitude for any occasion, and who actually seemed to *like* Kate.

As long as she had Elizabeth, Kate felt OK being at Columbia, far away from home, far away from Adam. She had someone to eat meals with, to walk to the bookstore with, someone to study with. And even though Kate wasn't nearly as talkative as Elizabeth, she never felt awkward or stupid. Maybe Elizabeth somehow knew that Kate was busy taking it all in, seeing how open and friendly Elizabeth was to *everyone* and how much they all liked Elizabeth in return. And that was part of the problem. Everyone else wanted Elizabeth, too. She was constantly being invited out to things—parties, meals off campus, movies. And it became obvious that Kate didn't, or couldn't, fit in with Elizabeth's other friends. Finally, after a couple of months of feeling like the fifth wheel at every outing, and after her falling-out with Adam, Kate asked Elizabeth for help.

"You know, I think I finally figured out what I want," she mentioned to Elizabeth casually one night, when they were both getting ready for bed. In the safety of the dark, Kate was able to say, "I couldn't really bring a whole wardrobe with me, so I think I need to get some things." She could tell Elizabeth was excited to help her. She had been more than generous with offering to let Kate borrow whatever she wanted. Kate always declined, not wanting to accidently ruin any of Elizabeth's things.

"We can find some great stuff downtown!" Elizabeth had said excitedly. "Just a few things, you know, to accessorize what you already have."

That weekend Elizabeth introduced Kate to the Greenwich Village shops along Broadway, picking up cute skirts and tops at Unique Boutique, Canal Jeans, and Le Chateau. Even the Gap was more fun to shop in with Elizabeth there to pick out the right cuts and colors for Kate, who finally figured out that she'd been wearing clothes two sizes too big. And even with the modest budget provided by her part-time job at the library, Kate felt like she had a brand-new wardrobe.

"I want to cut my hair, too," Kate said as they passed a salon. It was all one length and to her waist now, and she still wore it in a braid all the time—far from the just-below-the-shoulder layered cuts that all the other girls, including Elizabeth, wore.

"What?! Your hair is gorgeous," Elizabeth protested. "I

would kill to have hair that shiny."

"I need a change," Kate insisted. "This place takes walk-ins."

Elizabeth turned Kate away from the salon window by her shoulders. "Are you sure?"

"Positive."

"Then we're going to do this right. I'll call my stylist, who I've been going to for forever. If he can get my mass of curls to look halfway decent, you're going to be a knockout." Elizabeth smiled. "Not that you aren't already."

They headed uptown, and Kate was immediately struck by how fancy the salon was, the way they offered her *sparkling* water upon entrance and offered her a robe to wear. The staff gushed over Elizabeth, how they had missed her coming in for her biweekly manicure. An over-tanned man with shockingly white hair and a silver earring came over and twirled a lock of Kate's hair around his finger. "This is the girl you were telling me about?"

As if sensing Kate's discomfort over the attention, not to mention the impending price tag of a stylish cut, Elizabeth said, "I know—can you imagine wanting to cut off such fabulous hair? I convinced her to at least let me treat her to my favorite salon." She winked at Kate then, and Kate was reassured that Elizabeth would take care of everything. Which she did—as the stylist brushed Kate's hair out of its braid, which was no easy feat given its length and thickness, Elizabeth directed him to keep it long. "It's your signature look," she said to Kate.

The stylist nodded and continued to brush. "How long has it been since your last cut?"

Kate thought for a moment and felt herself flush. It certainly was before her father moved out, since he was the always the one who cut it, and even so, he would only trim it once a year or so. So it had been at least three years. "Ummm, not sure. A … long time. Just never seemed to have a chance to get around to it."

"It's beautiful," the stylist reassured her. "You're like Rapunzel!" He placed his hands on her shoulders and looked at her in the mirror. "We'll just clean it up a bit to make it a little more … modern," he smiled. He cut her hair so that it hit well below her shoulders, with plenty of layers for fullness and style. Shorter layers around her face framed her cheekbones.

From then on, Kate was amazed at what the right hair and clothes could do for her. She felt more confident, lighter even, without the baggy clothes and miles of hair weighing her down. She didn't come out of her shy shell overnight by any means, but the boost of confidence helped to convince her to go out more with Elizabeth and her friends. And there were always those times they would hit a nearby karaoke bar, where Kate had never felt more confident than when she was belting out a popular tune, earning the admiration of her newfound friends. She had always had a good voice, but with a new look, a new attitude, and new friends, she was no longer the glee club geek.

Kate and Elizabeth lived together all four years of college, but during sophomore year Elizabeth met her soul mate in her now-husband, so they spent less time together. When Elizabeth got married ten years ago, hers had been the only wedding Kate had ever been a bridesmaid in, and it was still one of the only weddings where Kate had not been relegated to a singles table on the outskirts of the reception as some second-tier guest.

Kate prized her friendship with Elizabeth still, considered it comparable to her current three girlfriends, who were *her* soul mates. She felt a little guilty for not telling Elizabeth about the true nature of her engagement, but she had promised Alberto she would keep their inner circle as small as possible.

She noticed a message from Adam pop up on the screen— it was just like him to respond right away, since he was the type to constantly have some device at his fingertips.

Coming to NYC. Would love to catch up.

Chapter 4

It took work to keep her size two figure, so on Monday morning, Kate was back to her daily running routine, starting at 5:30 a.m. By 7 a.m., she was at her desk, just as she was every weekday morning, dressed in her uniform—hair pulled back in a sleek chignon, minimal eye makeup, red lipstick, wearing a fitted sheath dress and stilettos. Yes, she knew she looked like a shark. Her uniform was her armor and helped her cultivate her reputation for severity. She wasn't here to make friends, just money.

The market had swung up and down that day, unfortunately ending down. By 7 p.m., she was exhausted on the walk back to her apartment. She picked up some dinner and a bottle of wine on the way, just as she always did, since there was nothing in her refrigerator except bottles of water. As she ate in front of her computer a little while later, she contemplated going to the gym in her building to do some weights. But then she saw Alberto pop up on chat and decided that having him over would be a much more fun workout.

Thankfully there were few gigs booked for Monday nights, and Alberto took barely any time at all to arrive from his place in Brooklyn. They barely greeted each other, both clearly knowing what Kate called him over for. As she lifted his shirt over his head, she thought what a great way this was to forget about how much money had been lost that day.

A little while later, she was still in bed, answering work emails while Alberto got dressed. This was one of the things she adored about him—they were just so compatible with each other's needs: a good romp in bed without the need for snuggling or small talk afterward. She put down her iPhone long enough to accept the kiss on the cheek he gave her and to tell him that she would go to his show on Friday night. Alberto took a sip of her wine before letting himself out, and as she heard the door shut behind him and settled back into her pillows, Kate thought again just how perfect this arrangement was.

By Wednesday, the market had picked up, and so had everyone's mood. Kate was looking forward to seeing Adam again, for the first time in years. His flight was delayed, so instead of meeting her for dinner with all her friends, she planned to meet him for a drink at his hotel instead.

After work, she stopped at home for a quick change and to shake out her tightly pulled back hair so that it fell in soft waves around her shoulders. She pulled on a mini skirt and sequined tank top with a pair of strappy sandal stilettos. With all the heels she wore, one would think she had a height complex, but at five foot nine barefoot, she really just liked the way they looked.

In the cab ride on the way to Cafeteria in Chelsea, Kate remembered to put on her ring. When she arrived, she spotted Cass, Nick, and Suzanne already seated at a table and joined them just as the waiter was bringing their drinks. The very cute waiter. She flashed him a smile and ordered her usual dirty martini. "Very dirty," she said huskily.

After he left, Suzanne laughed. "Do you ever turn it off?"

"Now what fun would that be?"

Mia wound her way to their table a few moments later, almost crashing into a waiter who apparently didn't see her. Much as she loved her friend, Kate sometimes wished Mia didn't present herself so *invisibly*. Tonight she was wearing black pants, a grey top, and sensible mid-heel black sandals. Kate was pleasantly surprised that she was able to make it tonight since she often cited the hip Chelsea scene as "not for her" and preferred to stay home. If she didn't already have a soon-to-be live-in boyfriend, she might have been a good hookup for Adam.

Kate looked around and thought of Adam then. It was probably for the best that he hadn't been able to make it to dinner. This sort of place wasn't for him either—loud and trendy—and she certainly wanted him to have a good time while he was here. Yes, it was better that they just meet for a drink later.

"So your friend Adam is coming?" Suzanne asked. "What's he like?"

"We've never met any of your friends from Michigan; I'm so curious!" Mia chimed in. "Is he going to share your secret past?"

Cass gasped in mock revelation, picking up on Mia's cue. "You lost your virginity to him, didn't you? That's why he's so special." They all laughed then, even Nick, who shook his head a little. If he and Kate hadn't been friends since college, it may have been awkward, but as it was, he was glad to be included in the occasional dinner.

"Ugh, hardly!" Kate laughed. The thought of sex with Adam … well, he'd been not quite like a brother back in high school, but certainly not anything close to a romantic interest. He had been a fixture in her life, just a constant presence, neither romantic nor unromantic. "Adam was my rock. I didn't have that many friends in high school." Hardly any at all. "Adam was just always around to do homework with or see a movie. We were pretty nerdy together, quite honestly!"

"Ever since we've known you, you've been some sort of a financial wizard, a man magnet, and major party girl—"

"Don't forget great friend," Kate interrupted Mia. "I'm very complex." She said it jokingly, but she truly felt that there were few others who understood her. She also hardly ever talked about anyone from home, except a little bit about her parents. So it was natural that they would be curious about anyone from her past.

"Adam and I just … lost touch," Kate continued.

She didn't really like to think about that night when she had gone to visit him at Stanford. It had hurt that he had been so harsh. It had hurt more that he'd been right.

"It'll be great to see him again even after all this time. There's just such a familiarity with people that you grew up with, you know? We've both changed, I think; we're totally different people now—at least I am. But we have all that history—I'm sure we'll have tons to talk about."

"Legacy Friends," Cass said. "You'd probably never have noticed him now, but since you were friends before, you'll stay friends now."

To say that Kate would not have noticed Adam had they met now would not have been entirely accurate. The bar at the Tribeca Grand where Adam was staying would often attract a pretty fancy crowd in the evenings—a mix of trendy and financial types, young women in short dresses, young men in slim-cut suits. It would have been difficult not to notice Adam at the end of the bar, alone, nursing a beer, wearing a white T-shirt that quite possibly came in a three pack, a pair of jeans that had seen better days, and flip-flops. Kate smiled. He looked so ... California ... and yet his sandy blond hair that was too long in the front, and the slightly downturned corner of his eyes that made his natural expression slightly sad—it was so familiar and so Adam.

She snuck up behind him and whispered, "Can I buy you a drink?"

Adam turned and grinned, knowing it was her right away. He stood to greet her, and she had to admit she was a little bit wowed. She knew she had changed a lot since their friendship, both inside and out. And it was apparent that Adam had changed a great deal as well. When she had run into him while in college, she had noticed he was taller, but now he wasn't quite so skinny—still on the slender side, definitely, but nowhere near the scrawny teenager he had been. He stood taller as well, no longer hunching his shoulders forward. He had a great smile now, one that reached his blue eyes, erased any trace of unhappiness, and showed off his teeth, which he'd had straightened somewhere along the way. And he was *tan*—those Michigan winters did nothing for him, but apparently his condo in Maui did (she did follow his Facebook updates, after all).

"You look so California," she said, giving him a kiss on the cheek. It was odd to have to crane her neck up to do so since she was more than six feet tall in her shoes.

"You look so New York," he responded, taking in her outfit. He shook his head a little, and she wasn't sure if that was a compliment or not.

She slid onto the bar stool next to him, and before she even thought to get the attention of the waiter, Adam had already ordered for her. "She'll have what I'm having," he said.

"How do you know what I want?" she said, automatically defensive. She hadn't even thought about her drink order yet.

"You always want what I'm having," Adam smiled. "Always have."

Kate couldn't help but laugh. It was true after all. When they were in high school, she would constantly eat off his plate or munch on half his movie popcorn after saying she didn't want her own. And she had to admit, she didn't really feel like having another martini, and that amber lager in front of him looked pretty refreshing.

"So what are you doing in New York anyway? How long are you here for?" Kate asked. Beyond meeting tonight, they hadn't talked about why he was there or how long he was staying. She would certainly plan to spend some time with him before he had to go back home.

Adam took a sip of his beer and shrugged. "I have a few meetings set up. Not sure how long I'll be here, depends on how those go."

She tried to picture him in business meetings, shaking hands with clients, wearing a suit and tie, and found she couldn't. She *could* picture him dressed just as he was now, in front of a computer, with his wire-framed glasses. *That's what's different!* "Where are your glasses?" she exclaimed.

He laughed. "Lasik is the best invention ever."

They spent a little more time chatting, mostly over how much each other had changed, when Adam yawned. "I'm sorry. I didn't think I'd be this tired with the time difference and everything. The flight must have taken a lot out of me."

"It's OK," and it really was. Kate didn't take it personally that he was tired in her company; he was just Adam. "I have an early morning anyway, so we should probably call it a night."

Adam walked her out of the hotel and watched her leave after she declined the need for a cab or the offer for him to walk her home, which he did out of habit more than anything else.

Back in his room, he was tired, exhausted really, but unable to sleep. All these years, he hadn't known, or hadn't been willing to admit, how much he missed her. When he first heard her voice, it felt like a homecoming, cutting through the din of all that bar noise. When he turned around, sure, she looked different, but as soon as she sat down and did that thing where she twirled her hair with her finger, he saw the old Kate, his friend Katie. He swallowed the lump that had suddenly formed out of uncertainty for how he should handle this feeling, and out of guilt.

Claudia had been right after all, though he wouldn't admit it until this very moment. There had always been something between them, she had accused—something that kept their relationship from being as close as it should have been. He had thought he had been happy with her, had gladly handed over his credit card when they had gone engagement ring shopping together, had gamely signed the title deed on their house in Palo Alto, which had perfect floors made of sustainable bamboo and was located in the best school districts. He had supportively sat through hours of listening to her wedding guest list angst and genuinely was puzzled when she accused him of not caring enough, not having his heart in it, of acting like a robot with no emotions.

He certainly didn't lack for feelings now. They hadn't talked about Kate's engagement at all; she hadn't brought him up, hadn't brought him period, thank God. What would he have done if she had shown up with her *fiancé* in tow? It was bad enough that he saw that ring with every gesture she made. It made him feel like it was really too late, that after all this time, he had lost the chance with her that he hadn't even known he wanted.

But no, he told himself. She wasn't married yet. He wasn't big on breaking up anyone's relationship, but he knew better than anyone that being engaged wasn't the same thing as being married. And the fact remained—*she hadn't mentioned a word about him.* It was the right decision for him to come to New York, to see for himself. If she was happy, truly happy with this guy, whomever he may be, Adam would leave, he told himself. He would see her happiness for himself, as the old friend he was, looking out for her like he always had.

Chapter 5

The next afternoon, Kate was at work when she got a text from Adam:

Done with meetings and sick of hotel. Can I hang at your place?

She texted back:

Sure, front desk has extra key. I'll let them know you're coming.

Kate chuckled to herself. It was just like him to want to just hang out at home. Most people would want to take in the tourist sites during a rare trip to the city. She thought for a moment and then texted him again:

If you're still around, I get home a little after 7. I can get dinner on the way.

Adam texted:

Sounds good.

And it did. Unbeknownst to her, Adam actually had taken a lot of the day to see the city. He had walked all the way up to Herald Square and back, grabbing lunch and snacks along the way. It was nice to actually walk around and not be in a car all the time. He could see why so many people loved it here—the energy, the diversity. The last time he'd been here was years ago for a technology conference. He'd barely seen the outside of the conference center then and hadn't bothered to contact Kate. He had just started dating Claudia at the time, and Kate had never really entered his mind. This time was different. He hadn't lied exactly when he said he had meetings; it just so happened that the meetings were in California and he attended by Skype. It was true that he was sick of his hotel room, or more accurately that he would rather be at her place.

As the doorman let him into Kate's apartment, Adam got the distinct impression that it was not a common occurrence for a man, or anyone else, to be here when Kate wasn't. Did she spend most of her time at her fiancé's place? As he looked around, he was struck by how pristine everything was, as though it had either just been cleaned, or that no one was around that much. Adam frowned. There was no dust on her shelves, shelves that held no photos, just nondescript vases and knickknacks. Even her work space in front of her computer had papers neatly lined up in rows. It was as if she purposely hid any of her actual personality from would-be visitors.

But then he saw her bedroom. He wasn't being overly nosy, he told himself—the door was wide open. And he didn't go in, just stood in the doorway and saw evidence of the Kate he knew. Her running shoes were next to the door, alongside an overflowing basket of laundry. On top of the dresser was a neat stack of clothes that looked like they had just come back from a laundry service and had yet to be put away. A bunch of small purses in a variety of colors spilled out of a basket. A pair of bright blue high-heeled shoes peeked out of her closet door, as if they were trying to kick themselves out of confinement. And the bed—it looked like it had been slept in, and only by one person, the way the blanket was tossed aside just on the left. Adam couldn't remember exactly when it had started, but at some point he and Claudia spent every night together, even when they still maintained separate apartments.

He went back out to her living room, turned on the television and his laptop, and waited.

"Hi honey, I'm home," Kate joked as she clumsily staggered into her apartment with multiple bags of food from her favorite Indian restaurant. "I didn't know what you liked, so I got nearly everything on the menu." Adam got up to take the bags from her, and she went through her usual routine of dropping her work bag on the floor and her keys, ring, and phone in a little tray by the door.

"Do you always look like that when you go to work?" Adam remarked as they unloaded the food onto her little dining table. He didn't seem to be judgmental, just curious. Kate laughed a little, noticing how different they looked—she in her usual chignon, full makeup, fitted skirt, and stilettos; he with his hair in his eyes, wearing a grey crewneck T-shirt with some logo across the chest of a company she'd never heard of, and jeans that may well have been the same ones he wore last night. He was barefoot, having left his flip-flops by the door.

"Always," she replied. "But I would probably be more comfortable chowing down on all this food if I changed." Kate went into her bedroom, threw her work clothes in the pile designated for dry cleaning, and put on her usual loungewear: a jersey knit tank top with matching shorts. She had washed the city grime off her face and was pulling her hair back into a loose braid as she walked barefoot out to have dinner.

"It's a complete transformation!" Adam said when he looked up from trying to find plates.

She went to get the plates herself, closing all the cabinet doors that he had left open in his search. "Sorry, I'm not trying to impress you," she smiled and gave him a mock "model pose" with her hand behind her head and lips pursed.

"Clearly not," Adam said under his breath and turned his back to her to go sit at the table.

Did I offend him? Kate wondered. She felt a little bad about her casualness. Adam had never been one to have a lot of girlfriends, and she just didn't picture him as the guy picking up a girl at a bar, or even a guy that girls flirted with. She didn't know anything about his breakup with his ex—what was her name, it started with a C. Maybe whatever happened with her made him sensitive about his boy-next-door vibe.

Kate poured each of them a glass of wine, thinking how nice it was that she wouldn't have to worry about trying to recork the leftover at the end of the meal. They started by each talking about their days—of course, Adam was never big on details, but she gathered that he had gotten around the city some. She

35

eventually felt comfortable enough to ask about his ex—she had to admit to some curiosity over this woman who had caught, and possibly broken, his heart.

They continued to eat—and drink—while Adam told her about Claudia. She was the sister of a friend he had started up a company with, and had come to bring them dinner on one of the many nights they worked late at his friend's apartment. "Pretty soon she was coming by all the time, and then we started dating. We got engaged, but then it didn't work out." He pressed his lips into a thin line and looked down at his food. "It was for the best."

"Are you still friends?"

Adam shook his head, still keeping his gaze down.

"Are you still friends with her brother?"

Adam shrugged and took a large bite of chicken, as if to avoid answering. He had never been one to talk about his feelings. Still, Kate felt like he was being extra closed off. Maybe she had been reading this wrong, and he didn't feel that old "legacy friend" comfort and closeness that she felt. Or maybe this Claudia really did a number on him and he was still battered from it.

"So what about you?" he asked when he was finally done chewing and had swallowed. "Tell me about the guy you're marrying."

Kate needed a big gulp of wine for this one. It was a perfectly reasonable question—she just hadn't been prepared to answer. "Well, he's a guy from school," she began. She ripped off another piece of naan, dipped it in some mango chutney, and chewed slowly.

"You told me that already," Adam said, watching her closely.

Kate had thought she would continue along with her usual storyline, as if Adam was just any other friend. But he wasn't. He was her oldest friend, and had been her closest and dearest for a long time. Sure, it was a long time ago, but seeing him again last night and then today made all those feelings come back again. There was nothing she couldn't tell him then, and she still trusted him now. "He's a good friend," she continued.

"I should hope so." Adam sat back in his chair now, waiting for her to finish speaking.

There was no turning back now. It was obvious that Adam knew something was off about her "engagement." And she'd certainly had enough wine to loosen her tongue a little. So she spilled it—it wasn't a very long or complicated story. She even told him that she and Alberto slept together sometimes, so it wasn't like he was a stranger to her. At that detail, Adam flushed a little, and Kate had to remember that sex just wasn't one of the things they used to talk about. "Just don't tell Linda. Or your family," Kate concluded.

"I won't," Adam said, glancing away. "You know I don't talk to my family."

His brow furrowed ever so slightly as he ran his hand through his hair. And there it was again: that look of a little sadness and vulnerability that reminded her of her high school best friend. Adam was the youngest of five brothers, with a stay-at-home mom and a dad who worked long hours but still took the boys to ball games on weekends. But his was far from the idyllic big family life that Kate had always wished for as an only child. Adam was the youngest, the smallest, the smartest, and his mother's favorite, which meant he was belittled and beaten up by his meathead brothers. Even his father thought he had been too "coddled" by his mother, was outwardly disappointed when Adam didn't have the physique or interest in playing football the way the rest of the "Ward Men" did. Adam's home life was constantly tense, and it didn't even end when his brothers graduated from high school. They had all gone to local colleges or trade schools, found local jobs and local girls to marry, and were "home" at their parents' house all the time. His entire family was relieved when Adam decided to go to Stanford for college.

Kate and Adam moved to the sofa to finish their wine. "Are you sure you know what you're doing with this whole marriage thing?" Adam asked. Surprisingly, Kate didn't feel annoyed with the way he questioned her judgment.

"I don't see myself getting married for the traditional reasons," she answered. "I don't see myself wanting kids. I don't even see myself being monogamous, quite frankly. Going downtown to sign a marriage certificate to help out a friend is as good a reason as any as far as I see it." Adam frowned slightly. "I'm not like other women, I know that. And as diverse as this city is, I'm still in a pretty traditional career field. It helps to have people think my personal life is becoming more traditional, too." She wasn't sure if he would understand this part and continued on, explaining how their boss would invite other colleagues to kids' birthday parties or other family-oriented events in an attempt to show a well-balanced work atmosphere, but how he would exclude her, saying he was sure she had more exciting things to do. And of course, she did have more exciting things to do, but she also missed on the career networking and face time that she felt gave others a leg up.

"My boss hosts a dinner every quarter as a thank-you to the spouses and significant others who support the long hours of his employees. Now that I have a fiancé, I get to go." The fact that her boss was actually a jerk who used these events as an excuse to justify his irrational demands on the job and just seemed to enjoy a certain amount of brownnosing was moot. Alberto was going to help her get an in with the boss.

Adam was still silent during her whole explanation. She wished he would say something. Was he disappointed in her? Surely he understood how much her career meant to her. "You know what the business world is like. Appearances count."

"It seems like you've thought about this a lot," he finally said.

"Well, not at first." Had she admitted that out loud before? "At first it was just something I put out there when Alberto was telling me about his visa expiring. But then the more I thought about it, the better it sounded. And then I bought some ring from a street vendor in the Village. And all of a sudden, I was the topic of conversation at work—in a good way!"

Adam nodded. "I just hope this works out the way you want it to."

"It will," she said, partly to him, partly to herself. "He hasn't pushed me into this, if that's what you think."

"I don't think that. I don't think anyone could push you

into anything." He smiled and looked directly at her then, and the tenderness in his blue eyes pierced her.

How did he still know her so well? "If I change my mind, it'll be fine. Alberto will be fine, and we would still be friends. I know what I'm doing."

Adam nodded again. "You always seem to."

They finished the wine and realized it was getting late. "I've got my run in the morning," Kate yawned.

"Mind if I join you?"

"Since when do you run?"

"There's a lot you don't know about me." His lips quirked up in a challenging smirk.

"I'm out the door at 5:30 sharp."

"Meet you in the lobby."

"You're really here," Kate mumbled when she saw Adam waiting for her in the lobby. "At least you aren't wearing flip-flops."

"Good morning to you too, Sunshine," Adam said brightly. She was still not a morning person apparently.

"Are you still on West Coast time or something?"

"I don't need a lot of sleep, remember?"

She responded with something like a grunt and headed out the door, leaving Adam to follow her. Once outside, she said, "I'm used to running alone." She put her earphones in her ears. "I like to run alone."

Adam just smiled. "No problem." He started to jog, just a couple of paces behind her, watching the swing of her braid side to side, enjoying the rhythm as she hit her stride. He was happy to give her the space and simply enjoyed being near her. She had good running form—he guessed they both became a little more athletic after high school somehow. He gulped, watching her behind, trying not to think *too many* dirty thoughts. It was the same last night after she had changed out of her work clothes—had she even been wearing a bra? It was different for him to be thinking of her this way. Yet he couldn't help it. She had been his best friend, and now? He wanted more. Definitely more.

Hearing her side of the engagement story was tough for him last night. He wasn't sure if he should be happy that she wasn't in love with someone else or sad for her that she didn't think she'd find love for herself. When had she become so jaded? She really thought she had a great life, the high-powered career, going out all the time, hooking up with a new man every week. He tried not to think about the men. Was she happy?

He stood next to her at a corner as they waited for a light. She glanced at him, as if to say, "You're still here?" He just smiled at her again. Those laps he did in the pool every so often apparently came in handy toward building some endurance.

They continued on their run. The looks Kate got from other morning runners were not lost on Adam, particularly the ones from other men, young or old. Adam glared at them and realized something. If not this Alberto guy and his need for a green card, then someone else. Some other guy, *not Adam*, could be the one who convinced Kate that there was more to life, more to love, than a one-night stand. He hated this possibility, hated it more than the possibility that she might actually be married in a few months.

By the time they returned to her building, she was in a much better mood. He was a lot more winded than she was, which added to her amusement. "Still competitive," he panted.

"You held your own," she said, barely out of breath with her hands on her hips. "I'm impressed."

"I'll get better at this."

"Planning to come along again?"

"I'm thinking I might stay in town for a while." He paused to catch his breath and see her reaction. She didn't seem unhappy with the news, but not jumping for joy either. "My meetings have gone well. I need to jump on the opportunity while I can."

She smiled. "I'll see you tonight then?" She turned toward the elevator after he gave her a nod.

Chapter 6

It was Friday evening, and Kate was in a foul mood. It was her boss's fault. OK, the market closed in a god-awful low. So everyone in the office had a right to be in a foul mood. But the MD was being a complete jerk, making the team stay late to brainstorm how they were going to get more investors and more money, just because his own wife and kids happened to be out of town and he had nothing better to do.

Adam texted her:

Dinner tonight?

Kate responded:

Stuck at work

She had been looking forward to dinner and then heading down to Alberto's show afterward. She still wasn't sure how long Adam was going to be in town—he was elusive about that and apparently had few enough commitments at home that he was keeping his trip open-ended. But now she was stuck in a conference room, staring across a table at a bunch of other people who all would rather be somewhere else, while their managing director drew on a white board. She wasn't at this firm to make friends and didn't believe she could really have friends at work—it was just too competitive. But sometimes she liked to look around a room like this and imagine the lives of her colleagues.

There was Jim, the classic Wall Street type in a well-cut suit, with a house in Connecticut, a stay-at-home wife, and two children. He would have called his wife hours ago to say that he wouldn't make it to date night/soccer practice/ neighborhood barbecue.

Stephen was next to him, an older version of the same, whose kids were now out of the house and who only called him for money. It was well-known within the firm that he was having an affair with one of the investor relations girls, who was barely older than his kids. The MD practically gave him a slap on the back in encouragement when those rumors came out—and he also used the information to guilt Stephen to do his bidding.

There were three lap dogs, as Kate liked to refer to them. Recent MBA grads who were hungry—hungry for approval, hungry to be able to pay off their student loans, hungry for the next promotion. She had been one of them herself not that long ago, and she felt for them. They were still trying to figure out their lives, how to balance the demanding work hours with their desire for a social life. Kate was fairly certain the woman had a serious boyfriend. She would be trying to figure out how to balance work with her desire for a family. She would be trying too hard to figure out her life's priorities. It would take them a few years, just as it had taken her. At least one of them would quit for a lower pressure job with fewer hours, in an attempt to have a relationship.

And then there were the mid-level women, just herself and Rachel, who was several years older than she was. Rachel was hardly competition, though, having taken herself out of the workforce for a couple of years when her kids were younger. Kate did not want to be Rachel at all, looking at her watch every few minutes, while she missed something at home. Their MD would sometimes make snide comments to Rachel if she asked for time off, asking if she had something better to do, or would her stay-at-home husband be able to handle things for her?

Kate sometimes wondered what her colleagues thought of her. She tried not to give them too much information, thus the daily uniform, the shark exterior. The more their MD tried to socialize with her, the more closed she had become, seeing how he used personal information against the others. So then she decided that her colleagues would only know what she wanted them to know. At first, it behooved her to be somewhat of the party girl at the office because her MD thought she was "fun." She never really showed her true self, never flirted around colleagues or anything like that. But her willingness to go to a strip club with male colleagues and clients was somehow considered an asset to the firm. More recently, though, she felt like her fun status hindered her career trajectory, so her engagement came at the right time.

She sat straighter in her seat. She was still hungry like the lap dogs. She had just learned a thing or two over the years that could help her stand out without having to stomach being a constant brownnoser. Let her boss think that she was settling down now, that she needed to continue to be a breadwinner, no, a *rainmaker*, in order to support herself or to pay for an extravagant wedding. She nodded at whatever it was the boss was saying, staring at his white board diagram as if there was nothing better than sitting in this room on a Friday night. The boss at least took notice and actually made eye contact with her when he said excitedly, "See, you get it! That's the key here in this little downturn."

Little downturn? It's another recession, you idiot. She smiled brightly.

"Fear and Greed," the boss said. "Now our clients are in a state of fear. We've got to get back to greed."

Finally, *finally*, an hour and a half later, they were released.

Kate decided to stop home to quickly change her clothes and was surprised that Adam was still there. It reminded her a bit of high school, when she would come home late from glee club practice and he would be hanging out in her kitchen with her dad in order to escape his own family. She headed to her bedroom to change into jeans and a tank top. There was no time to do her hair, really, so she just brushed it out and pulled it into a high, loose bun. "You want to come with to see Alberto's band?" she called out to Adam. "I'm meeting some friends there—they want to meet you!" She came out to the living room to hear his response. "What kind of place is it?

Should I change?" he asked.

Kate smiled. He was in a pair of jeans and an old T-shirt. "Aside from the fact that New York men don't wear flip-flops, you're actually dressed completely appropriately. This place is a total dive."

Adam chuckled. "Should I be insulted?"

"You know what I mean," Kate said, swatting him playfully. It really was nice having him around. She went to grab a clutch from her closet, along with a pair of casual kitten heel sandals that she wouldn't be able to wear much longer once fall weather arrived.

When Kate and Adam arrived, Nick, Mia, David, and Suzanne were already there, at the table that Alberto reserved for her. The club was far from packed, but Kate always enjoyed a table front and center. Kate introduced Adam and was immediately glad that his first meeting with her closest friends (minus Cass, who had a rehearsal dinner tonight) was at a casual place where Adam clearly felt comfortable. They got a couple of pitchers of beer for the table, and Kate dove into the wings and chips, having skipped dinner for her meeting. Suzanne leaned into her. "He's kinda cute."

"Who?" Kate looked around. She'd met plenty of guys at Alberto's shows; this wouldn't be the first time.

"Adam," Suzanne replied.

Kate looked over at Adam, who was absorbed in some conversation with Nick and David that she couldn't hear but was apparently very entertaining. "Really?" she said back to Suzanne. "Are you interested? I thought you were dating that guy you met online, but hey, you know my motto—" Rule Number Three— manage men like money. Take a portfolio approach and don't put your emotions or your dollars in one basket. Where one investment fails, you've still got others.

"No," Suzanne replied, "but I don't think it would matter even if I were."

"What are you talking about?" Suzanne shrugged and then took an exaggeratedly long swig of her beer while she wiggled her eyebrows. "Stop speaking in riddles!"

At that moment, Alberto's band came on and all conversation stopped for cheering and music. Kate had always enjoyed his performances—maybe the former performer in her was a little envious that he had the guts and talent to pursue his dream. She could never have lived the life he did, though, not knowing when the next paycheck would come in, eating ramen noodles and eggs for weeks on end sometimes. And even if Kate could stomach the lack of security, the lack of control over her day-to-day life, she certainly couldn't stomach the nagging from Linda that she would surely incur with such a lifestyle. And she had to face facts: even if she had the moxie, she never *quite* had the talent. It sometimes hurt back in high school when Linda reminded her (repeatedly) that singing was a hobby, not a profession, and that glee club was only there to bolster her college applications, which would ultimately pave the way to a better (richer) future. Kate never argued with Linda about it back then, knowing she was right.

Kate caught Alberto's gaze as he sang and played his guitar. He was handsome, no doubt about it, could probably find a number of women to marry him. She looked over at Adam again. He seemed to be enjoying the music as well, relaxing against the back of his chair, not taking his eyes off the band while he drank his beer. It often annoyed her when groups of people would continue their chatting, just getting louder and louder as the evening and beer wore on. Sure, it was a divey club and the band barely made any money from this show, but Alberto's original music had not been written strictly for the sake of being their background noise.

A couple of songs in, the crowd was starting to get livelier. Kate caught the eye of a guy at the next table and smiled. She checked for a wedding ring—none. She checked for a nearby girlfriend—none. She smiled wider and was about to get up when he broke eye contact. Then she noticed that Adam had draped his arm around the back of her chair. She let out a low sigh. She hadn't thought of Adam as a cockblock, and Suzanne had that weird smirk on her face again. *Oh well.* Adam wouldn't be around forever. She'd just get back her game when he was gone.

Chapter 7

This wasn't going to be easy, Adam realized. It was Monday and he had decided to fix up Kate's computer while she was at work. Simple projects like upgrading memory and installing a new hard drive had always relaxed him when he had other things on his mind. He was still trying to figure her out. He'd had lots of glimpses of the old Kate that he loved as his friend—the singing in the shower after the daily morning run made him laugh out loud with nostalgia the first time he heard her. Even her grumpiness in the morning, when she acted surprised to see him at 5:30 a.m., made him smile. Was it love, then, that he thought her grumpiness was cute? Or was he just satisfied that he was showing enough endurance to accompany her on a daily run at such a ridiculously early hour? *That* is what some would call love. He had a lot of respect for such discipline; she hadn't skipped a run since he'd been here, not even over the weekend after late nights with her friends.

She seemed to certainly apply this discipline to her work, which was something he didn't quite get. He understood ambition and her desire for success. What he didn't understand was the coldness—in the way she dressed, the way she talked about her coworkers. She was unapproachable on purpose. It was so different from the way she was with her other friends, from the way she was with him.

Adam guessed it had to do with Linda. She had long been a well-respected finance professor at the University of Michigan and would often make comments to Kate about the need for financial independence, the importance of having a career. There was one day when Linda had driven the two of them through a not-so-great neighborhood with unkempt houses and lawns, probably on the way to some math team competition. "This is where you'd be if I didn't work like I do," Linda had said to Kate. He tried to pretend like he hadn't heard the comment from the backseat; after all, his own neighborhood was only a notch better. But comments like that had to have had an impact on Kate's decision to pursue the kind of career that she chose, and in the manner in which she pursued it.

It was as if she felt like she had to choose one extreme or the other, Adam mused. Either become a frustrated performer in the arts like her father was a frustrated writer or become a relentless financial shark. Her personal life was the more or less happy medium, though she still didn't give herself enough credit to be able to have a real relationship. Adam wondered if her parents' divorce did more damage than Kate was willing to admit. How should a kid take it when her mother told her she was moving out because Kate was old enough to take care of herself now? That she no longer needed both parents at the ripe old age of sixteen?

Adam let out a long sigh. Complicated woman. His friends would have told him to steer clear, to not bother with someone with so much emotional baggage. But he couldn't. Kate's mere presence got under his skin, made his heart beat faster. Whether it was just the two of them in her apartment having dinner or when he was having to glare at that guy at the club, he wanted to be with her.

Alberto's presence was another complication. Adam believed Kate's story about the impending marriage. But there was still no doubt that Alberto was Kate's *type*. Struggling artist, but a good performer, Adam had to admit. They were entering into a marriage of convenience, sure, but then what? Maybe he would move in with her to save money? She already admitted to sleeping with him—and enjoying it. Adam scowled. She could be on her way to a real marriage. He almost wished he could call one of the guys back home, to get some perspective, maybe

47

help him see clearly and get his head on straight. But there was no way. His friends were Claudia's friends now, or they were married to Claudia's friends. And with the way he left things with her, had left their home and life that they were building together—well, it seemed fair that she get to keep their friends.

There was no doubt Kate clouded his judgment. Here he was in New York after all, for who knows how long, putting off various business requests for his return. Surely his friends would just tell him to forget her, to come back to his life in Palo Alto.

The more he thought about that life, the more he thought he needed a change. There was nothing *wrong* with that life. He liked mentoring and helping out these smart kids with great ideas. He liked helping them with their pitches for funding, for getting them to the next step in their development work. What he didn't like was the personal life that he spent so long building and then caused to crash around him. His friends thought he was having some early midlife crisis (because he was too old for a quarter-life one, as Claudia said). They couldn't understand why he chose to live in a tiny apartment again, eating pizza and takeout, living the bachelor life that they thought he'd been so happy to leave behind. In so many ways, he was a simple guy, with simple needs, happy to go along with whatever Claudia had planned for them. But then he realized what his life was lacking—and it was color.

He wanted the vibrancy again, to feel as energized about his personal life as he did about his work. He had tried to explain this to Claudia, but she just couldn't understand why he'd want to do things like go all the way into San Francisco to hang out in a crowded bar or club when they could just have all their friends over to their house for an evening of wine and cheese. Adam felt that flush of guilt all over again. She had accused him of changing on her, how he hadn't wanted anything different during the years they were together, but now suddenly they were supposed to get married and he was getting cold feet, finding excuses.

Maybe he had been trying to find excuses. Because if he was honest with himself, an evening in with wine and cheese sounded great—it sounded great if it was Kate he was with. Because she brought the color and vibrancy with her, and she always had. He tried to imagine his current California life with Kate. He could easily picture her there—a bit too easily. Adam shook his head. He was ahead of himself here, a useful trait when planning the vision for a new tech start-up, completely useless when planning to seduce Kate. He was going to seduce her in a way that she'd never been seduced before, body and soul. She was going to fall in love with him. She just didn't know it yet.

First things first. Adam booted up Kate's computer and logged in to his e-mail. It was time to get back in touch with an old mentor of his, who was now at the Engineering school at Cooper Union. He set up a meeting for this afternoon and then texted Kate:

Come straight home after work, I'll handle dinner.

"I'm home," Kate called as she threw her bag on the floor of her apartment. "Are you really cooking?" she asked incredulously on her way to her bedroom to change out of her work clothes. She had to admit it had been nice to have Adam around to relax with. They'd even gotten into something of a routine that surprisingly didn't feel boring.

She padded out to her kitchen in her bare feet and peered over his shoulder. "Mahi mahi with mango salsa," he responded to her silent inquiry.

"Mmmm," she inhaled. "Is that coconut I smell?"

"Coconut rice."

She got out wine glasses and a bottle of red from the counter rack, closing cabinets and drawers along the way. "You're going to have to figure out where everything is in this place if you're going to keep cooking for me," she smiled.

"If I don't leave the drawer open—"

"You won't know you've looked there. Yeah, I know," she said. "I'm just kidding. You're probably not going to be cooking for me much longer."

"Actually, I have some news." Adam expertly plated the fish over mounds of rice. "It looks like I'm going to be in town for a while. A couple of months maybe."

"Oh yeah? What for? Where will you live?"

"Some business prospects are panning out, and I want to see where those go. I got an apartment on a month-to-month lease. Nothing fancy, just a studio."

"Oh wow, that's great. You've been busy. Where's the apartment?"

"Downstairs."

"You mean downstairs, as in, in my building, downstairs?"

"I was here already—I decided to pop into the leasing office this morning. Some good deals on rent right now; I hope you're not overpaying yours—"

"You got an apartment in my building?"

"Yeah, isn't that convenient? I'll meet you for a run, I'll make you dinner—"

"I guess so." Kate wasn't sure how she felt about this. It was one thing for Adam to be around because he was visiting, an opportunity to reconnect because they didn't see each other. Now he was going to be *living* here? She took a bite of fish with some salsa. Delicious. Well, having him around was nice in a lot of ways. "So you're not actually *working*, though. I mean, you have a job in California, right?"

"It's more like consulting. I've been doing my own thing for a little while."

"That sounds nice. You sure don't have the daily grind like I do."

"Why do you do it? Do you like it?"

"I do like the work. I don't like my firm."

"Or your boss."

"Hate the boss. Oh, but I got good news. That dinner I told you about, where he pretends to want to get to know his staff's significant others, is next week. I have to remember to tell Alberto. I've never been invited before!" Truly, Kate believed it was a pretty decent day at work. She was sure she got the invite because of her eagerness on Friday *and* because she was engaged.

It pierced Adam to hear her talk like this. To mention Alberto *and* how she needs to suck up to her idiot boss all in the same breath. He wanted to pull her to him, to whisper against her ear, *Don't do this. Don't get married. Be yourself.* The way she'd pulled her hair back into a braid, wearing ratty yoga pants and a worn tank top, the way she took huge bites of food and licked her lips. It all reminded him of who she really was. Approachable, lovable. Of course, he couldn't dwell on those lips too much, or he really would just grab her to him. He cleared his throat and tried to concentrate on his food. *Doesn't she ever wear a bra at home?*

After dinner, Kate decided to get a drink with her friend Cassandra. She invited Adam along, but he declined. He did have some work to do—another Skype meeting actually—but really he knew he needed to give her some space. He could tell that she wasn't exactly thrilled about his new apartment being downstairs. But his plan called for proximity.

He bit his lip when she changed into a shiny tank top that barely had straps. Wouldn't she be cold? Her cropped pants hugged her curves like a second skin. And those "eff me" shoes—he stared hard at his computer, trying not to look up at her. "Have a nice time," he muttered.

Kate always made the effort to see Cass, whose work schedule didn't always mesh with others'. Suzanne was often on call, and Mia was a homebody—a thirty-year-old body with a fifty-year-old mentality. Maybe seventy-year-old, actually—Kate had no intention of being such a homebody at fifty.

Tonight they'd decided to meet at another newish bar that opened. Kate had been there before and she hoped it would make it through the recession. There was a decent crowd here, Kate was satisfied to see, and even more satisfied that Cass had snagged them a little table. She was not so young that standing three deep at the bar all night would suit her. Cass, of course, was in the middle of typing a message on her Blackberry and gave her a "one sec" sign. Kate wasn't the least bit offended, knowing full well that work often had to take precedence, and besides, it gave her a moment to scan the crowd. There were some cute guys here.

"So I hear you're living with a hottie who's not your husband-to-be," Cass said in greeting, as she tucked her phone back in that giant purse she carried everywhere.

"Shh, lower your voice," Kate responded in mock seriousness. "No need to advertise. Besides, Adam is hardly a hottie, and I'm not really living with him. He's just … hanging out … at my place. A lot."

"Not hot? Suzanne said he was 'gorgeous.'"

"What, are you interested? You're with Nick, remember, who happens to be a good friend of mine."

Cass rolled her eyes. "Not me, idiot."

"Suzanne then? I guess she is always on the lookout for someone. I hadn't really thought—"

Cass cut her off impatiently. "Suzanne says there was chemistry—between Adam and *you*."

"Oh, that's silly. That's just two people who have known each other for eons. Nothing sexual." The thought of her and Adam was truly preposterous. They were so platonic, he barely even looked at her. And he was well … just *so* not her type! Her type was one of those guys at the bar, one who kept glancing over to her table.

In a little while, the crowd got more energetic, more fun. She and Cass joined a handful of others in dancing toward the back of the bar. Poor Adam was stuck in her apartment—working and eating takeout was no New York experience. She decided to text him to meet them and gave him the address—she wanted Cass to see for herself how platonic they were, anyway. He didn't text her back right away; maybe he was asleep already, so she put her phone away.

Whether because of the great vibe or having had a few drinks, Kate and Cass made quick friends with three guys at the bar and decided to join them in a round of shots. It reminded Kate of how much fun she and all the girls had when they were all single, all carefree, before things like serious relationships and serious careers came into the picture. Cass was busy chatting with one of the guys who was about to get married—where was the venue, who was doing their music, how to get his fiancée to calm down about things. Kate looked over at the one she had noticed earlier in the evening, she thought he said his name was Will—or maybe Bill. She liked 'Will' better, so that's what she called him. She crooked her index finger toward her to draw him away from his friends a little. "So, Will, are you getting married too?"

He leaned into her. "Nope."

"Me either." He was a decent kisser, this 'Will,' and knew where to put his hands, considering they were in a crowded bar. On her hips, squeezing them a little. She couldn't stand when a guy started trying to run his hands down her ass or up her shirt in a public place. Oh, but now he was maybe a bit too eager, or just a bit too drunk. She did not enjoy being slobbered on. As luck would have it, she peeked out of the corner of her eye and spotted Adam. She was never so relieved to see him, to have an out from this guy who was starting to remind her of a golden retriever with his eagerness.

"Adam," she called out, but he had already spotted her and was scowling as he made his way through the crowd. Maybe he wasn't into this kind of bar scene. She went over to meet him. 'Will' still had his arm around her waist while she brought Adam over to their little group. "My friend Adam from Michigan," she introduced. "Oh, you probably say you're from California now, don't you? San Francisco or San Jose … one of those, right?" she said back to Adam. She babbled when she was drunk, she knew, so she just took another sip of her drink and whispered to Cass, "See? Not hot."

"Not everyone would agree." Cass pointed her drink behind Kate. A petite brunette was smiling at Adam and engaging him in some small talk. Quick work; she didn't waste any time, Kate approved.

"Suppose he's a catch for somebody," Kate murmured to Cass. "Just not for me."

They stayed for a few more drinks, a couple more shots,

until the crowd had really thinned. Adam seemed to be laughing and having a good time, and Kate was glad she invited him out. 'Will' gave her his number, which she pretended to put into her phone. The brunette wrote something on a napkin and slid it into Adam's back pocket. Did he ever wear pants that weren't denim?

Kate and Adam put Cass in a cab before walking together back to 'their' building.

"These fucking shoes," she scowled. "Either I'm drunk or my heel is loose."

Adam laughed. "I'm pretty sure it's the former."

"It has been a while since I drank that much." She tottered and he put his arm around her waist to steady her. "You always were my rock."

"Do you want to wear my flip-flops for the rest of the walk?"

She turned to glare at him, and he just smiled bemusedly. "Just walk slowly and keep your arm around my waist."

She poked an index finger at his stomach. "You're a rock all right. Your abs are like a rock." Was she starting to slur?

"You're drunk."

When they got to their building, Adam wanted to make sure she got to her apartment OK, and Kate didn't protest. "I'm spinning," she said after she flopped onto her bed. "Is the bed spinning?"

Adam brought her a glass of water and sat on the edge of her bed next to her. "No."

She held onto his forearm. "Are you sure?"

"Yes."

The next thing Kate knew, there was sunlight streaming through the window right onto her face. Her arm was thrown over the chest of a guy who was breathing softly next to her. Did she bring someone home? Oh, it's Adam. Right, he brought her home. They were fully clothed and on top of her blanket. How drunk was she? What time was it? At some point she remembered her alarm going off, but then it stopped, and she thought it was a dream. She remembered thinking she was too comfortable where she was to get up. She looked at the clock and bolted upright. 7:05 a.m.

"I'm late for work," she said loudly, a bit too loudly from the pulsing in her head. She held a hand to her forehead as she rushed into the shower. When she came out, Adam had rolled over onto his side, with his back toward her. "Don't turn around, I'm getting dressed," she said to him, just in case he was awake. He grunted in acknowledgement. She was fully alert and over her headache now—a five-minute shower could sometimes work wonders. "Did you turn off my alarm?"

"Didn't think you'd be in any shape to run today."

"I still need to get up for work," she said testily, pulling on the nearest dress that had recently been cleaned. She skipped the pantyhose and started on her makeup. There was no time to put her hair up as usual, so she just pulled it back into a tight, high ponytail on her way out the door.

Chapter 8

On the morning of "the big dinner," as Kate had taken to calling it, she was a bit more tense than usual. She had already spent a good part of the weekend emailing and texting Alberto, coaching him. Her stress showed in her run, Adam thought. Her pace was more regular, her posture rigid. Even her facial expression remained stoic. She didn't look around at all to enjoy the beautiful day, just straight ahead, thinking about how to make sure this "engagement" remained believable. When they got back from the run, she spoke of nothing else.

"If he says something that's off, I'll just chalk it up to translation. English isn't his first language, so I'll pass off any blunders ... Any shop talk, anything about business, Alberto is a star." And so on. If Adam didn't have the patience of a saint, if he wasn't half in love with her, he'd be irritated as hell. It was irritating enough that some other guy would be known as her husband-to-be.

After Kate got dressed in one of her usual uniforms and left for work and Adam put her discarded clothes into a laundry basket as had become his habit, he jumped in the shower himself. A nice, long shower was a relaxing way to end a run, and today he found it was a good way to clear his head. How would it be once she went public with Alberto? The dinner was only for work, he knew, but maybe it was her nerves about it that made Adam feel like this dinner made the engagement a big deal to Kate as well. That maybe it felt more legitimate in *Kate's* mind once she stepped out on his arm.

Adam dried himself off and wrapped a towel around his waist while he went to get himself a bottle of water. It really was a lot more comfortable to hang out at her place—he was still living with an air mattress and almost no other furniture while he figured out how long he would be in New York. The guest lecturer gig at Cooper Union was not a long-term project. And, well, if it didn't work out with Kate—and Adam hated to think of that possibility—there was no reason for him to stay.

The front door opened while Adam stood in the kitchen drinking his water.

"Forgot my ring," Kate explained, exasperated, almost to herself. "Of all the days—" She stared at him for a moment then, surprised he was half-naked, or surprised he was still in her apartment? He saw her swallow and did she flush ever so slightly? It was the former, he concluded satisfactorily. "You're showering here now?" she asked, clearly trying to cover her reaction.

"I like your smelly soaps," Adam deadpanned, not breaking her gaze.

"I'm late," she said.

Adam nodded.

He chuckled as he locked the door behind her. He'd get her yet, he thought; he would get under her skin as she had done to him. In her haste to leave, Adam noticed that she left her iPhone behind when she put it down to put on the ring. He paused for a moment. He knew it was wrong, but he couldn't resist. He picked it up and, of course, it prompted for a pass code. He paused for a moment. *What the hell, it's worth a shot.* He punched in "1111," the kind of code Kate would use as the easiest four digits to punch in. The phone unlocked. He let out a breath. *Note to self: talk to Kate about secure passwords.*

Well, there was no turning back now. She left her phone here—she *never* did that. Fate had dealt him a good hand, and he wasn't going to waste it. He easily navigated to the latest text exchange between Kate and Alberto. *Dinner is at Del Posto at 8 p.m.* Kate had texted.

Adam quickly tapped out a message:
Just found out, dinner cancelled. You're off the hook.

He didn't hit the send button just yet. Was he really doing this? Just then his own phone rang. Caller ID identified a 212 area code number that he didn't recognize, but he picked it up anyway. "Adam, it's me. Did I leave my phone at home?"

Adam swallowed guiltily, "Umm, let me check. Uh, yeah, it's here by the door."

Kate sighed, "Oh good, for a second I thought I lost it. Will you just keep it with you in case Alberto calls or something? My passcode is 1111 if you need it to check for messages."

"Uh, yeah, OK. You know, that's not very secure—"

"Just call me here at work if Alberto calls, OK?"

"Sure, no problem."

Adam exhaled after they hung up. She practically handed this opportunity to him, he told himself.

He hit the send button on the text to Alberto and then deleted the message history. 8 p.m. That gave him plenty of time.

After meeting with his former professor and mentor and sitting in on one of the undergraduate classes in the Engineering school, Adam headed uptown, to Fifth Avenue to do some shopping. It had been a while since he treated himself or even had any occasion to do so. It felt good, he had to admit. He could understand why Kate was so into getting dressed up to go anywhere, though he found her just as attractive when she was in her pj's as when she was dressed to the nines.

Adam arrived at Del Posto at five minutes to 8. He hadn't told Kate about the change in plans, knew she'd arranged to meet Alberto at 7:45, and didn't want her to have time to think too much about the switch. She'd sweat it out a little, but she'd be at her best if it happened naturally, if she didn't have time to prep herself or him.

She saw him right away, since she was nervously waiting for Alberto's arrival. She looked confused, of course, but Adam swiftly took her elbow before she could say anything and kissed her lightly on the lips as he whispered, "Slight change in plans." Then, in a normal tone in case any of her colleagues were around, he said, "Is everyone else seated already? We're not late, are we, darling?"

"N-no, we're not late," she stammered.

"You must be the fiancé!" Adam heard behind him. Kate introduced him to a woman named Rachel and her husband Dan, and just like that, there was no time for questions, just as Adam had planned.

As the four of them were escorted to their table, Kate leaned into him and whispered, "You look … perfect."

Adam suppressed his smile. He had a role to play, after all. "Armani always fits."

Chapter 9

It wasn't like Alberto to stand her up. Something big must have come up. And then of course there was the matter of her forgotten phone. He must have called or texted. She would have been more annoyed if Adam hadn't come to the rescue. He certainly looked the part that he needed to play. My God, she almost hadn't recognized him with his hair styled back from his forehead (it was *styled*!). His blue shirt set off the color of his eyes and gave them an intensity that was disarming. And that suit. It fit him perfectly. Clothes didn't make the man, but they could certainly make him—what? Hot? Kate shook her head. This was *Adam*, and she was thinking he was hot just because he was wearing an Armani suit? Just because she felt an unmistakable jolt when his lips brushed hers? It had been barely a whisper of a kiss, but her knees had buckled slightly at his touch. It was just the shock at seeing him, she told herself. She looked at his feet, not expecting his flip-flops, but certainly not expecting Prada. Was she imagining it or was he taller? She looked up at him quizzically, wondering just who this man was. And since when did he have such a strong jawline? He smiled at her like an adoring husband-to-be. She let out a breath. He'd play his part well enough.

Kate introduced Adam to the others—there were only ten of them since her boss liked to keep things "intimate." She began to relax as pleasantries were exchanged and no one seemed to think anything was amiss. And why would they? Adam looked exactly like the kind of guy a vice president in asset management would be with. Confident, successful, polished.

"Mr. Kate," her boss boomed, "sit here by me. I always like to make sure to get to know the newcomers."

Kate was relieved that she'd already told Adam about how her boss insisted on referring to spouses as "Mr. or Mrs. Employee First Name." Jim's wife, Claire, had attended dozens of company dinners and functions, their boss's kids' christenings and birthdays, and she was still "Mrs. Jim."

"So how did you two meet?" the boss asked. "In business school, did you say, Kate, at NYU?"

"Actually, it was in high school," Adam responded easily. "We rediscovered each other when I was in New York for business. It's been long distance since then, but not for too much longer." He looked at Kate and smiled warmly then. *God, he's good.* Adam then went on to engross the boss with talk about his businesses in California, the state of the technology industry, all things that Kate knew vaguely about from their sporadic emails, but didn't know until then that he was quite so … successful.

The rest of the table managed to chitchat among themselves while the boss seemed engrossed by whatever Adam was saying. But before long, Kate realized that they were just killing time until the boss moved on to the next item on his mental agenda. Kate had heard that he had a formula for these dinners, that he always asked the same kind of questions. She hoped that Adam overheard enough about how she prepped Alberto to follow the script.

Apparently he hadn't, but what Adam came up with was better. When the boss moved on to leisure topics, he was obviously impressed by Adam's familiarity with private jets and Pebble Beach golf courses. By the time they finished the appetizer course, Kate was relaxed enough to actually enjoy the great wine that had been ordered. She tried to keep herself from staring at Adam too much. His appearance tonight still boggled her mind. He was so—confident, cocky even. He was talking about the gaming industry again—that hot new game that just came out was developed by a company that he started? Was that a Rolex on his wrist? Kate wasn't sure what to make of this

Adam, wasn't sure how much of this he was making up. She wasn't sure she *liked* this Adam.

But it didn't matter because her boss sure liked him. "What about kids?" she heard her boss ask Adam. She had not been prepared for that question, and half expected Adam to start choking on his bite of lamb. It was just like her boss to switch from one topic to another, trying to catch people off guard with their answers. "Are you going to get our Katie knocked up right away and take her out of the office for months?" Everyone at the table seemed surprised at the brashness of the question—everyone except Rachel, Kate noticed, and she felt an unexpected rush of sympathy for her.

Yet again, Adam didn't miss a beat. "Kids are great," he said diplomatically, deliberately looking at Rachel and then back at their boss, "for some women. For others, just a distraction from life. They aren't for *Kate* and me." This was clearly the right answer for her boss, and if anyone else at the table felt offended, they dared not show it.

"That's a beautiful ring," Rachel said, clearly trying to get in on some conversation while changing the topic. "What is it, two carats?"

"Thanks," Kate responded. "Yes, it's something like that …"

"I actually wanted to get something bigger," Adam stepped in, "something *really* special. But Kate here is just Ms. Practicality, you know."

He sounds like such a jerk. Kate smiled meekly at Rachel as a form of apology for Adam. She felt better when the boss made some "atta boy" comment to Adam, though, and said something to him that no one else could hear. Did he really just *pat Adam on the back*? Kate had never seen him do that to anyone.

By the end of the meal—no dessert or coffee since no one wanted to prolong the dinner for any longer than necessary— Kate had declared her engagement debut a complete success. Alberto's no-show was a blessing in disguise—there was no way he would have done as well as Adam. Her star was on the rise in her boss's eyes, and any of her colleagues who may have dismissed her as a contender for senior VP had better look out.

It didn't matter that it was all Adam's doing or whether or not anything he said tonight was true. Kate knew how this game was played, and she was going to do whatever it took to win at it.

Each of the couples immediately took off in their own directions upon leaving the restaurant—the boss in his black town car, the other couples by taxi or on foot. Kate waited until she and Adam were out of earshot from anyone else before she unleashed her excitement.

"Oh my God, Adam, you were—"

"An asshole," he said, raising an eyebrow and smirking at her.

She laughed, "The *perfect* asshole! You were brilliant! I've never seen my boss like *anyone* before."

"Glad you're happy. That was the point."

Kate knew he had never been entirely on board this plan of hers. She stopped him on their walk and looked up at him. "Thank you," she said in all seriousness. This was the first chance she'd had to really look at him that night. His expression had softened since they left the restaurant, and she recognized the old Adam, *her* Adam underneath the polished look he prepped for tonight. The look he prepped for *her*. "I owe you big," she smiled.

"This job is really important to you. You're important to me," he replied. "You're welcome."

Kate started walking again. This wasn't the first time he'd commented about the importance of her job. "It's not a great firm," she started.

Adam huffed, obviously waiting for an opening to tell her what he really thought. "Tell me about it. That guy's a total jerk. And a moron!"

"I know, I know," Kate went on. "It's just not a great time to be in finance. It's not like I can just turn around and find something else!"

"Have you tried?"

"I'm so close to becoming a Senior VP; I can't start over someplace else," Kate defended. She wanted to make him understand, needed to make him understand. "When I got this job, Linda was so excited for me. She had no idea what it is that I actually did—she still has no idea. She just knows that it pays me well and that I won't get stuck like she did." This wasn't something that Kate would tell just anyone. But Adam knew her, and he knew her mother. He knew that Linda's one mantra to Kate all her life was that above all else, she needed financial security. *Money doesn't buy happiness*, Linda would say, *but you can't be happy if you're hungry.* Sure, Kate was a far cry from going hungry, but her own ambitions, her own desire to *be somebody* meant that she was going to put her all into whatever career she decided on. She wasn't going to get stuck at some mid-level, like those who were mommy-tracked. It was fine for them, but kids were so far off in the horizon of her own life that they would probably be a biological impossibility. "Linda didn't get tenure for a long time because of me." She halted him when he was about to correct her. "I know it's not my fault. I know she loves me. It's just a reality that she had to be a parent over being a professor for a while. I don't have any personal reasons that should hold me back from my career."

"Do you want to have personal reasons?" His tone was even, not judgmental, but inquisitive.

"I don't know," Kate said honestly. "I like the way my life is. I have fun, I have friends, I just don't feel like I need a life partner in the traditional sense. I'm perfectly capable on my own."

"I know you're independent and capable. I'm not talking about *need*," Adam corrected her. "I mean do you *want* a partner and a real relationship?"

It had been a long time since anyone asked her that, and a long time since she'd asked herself that. In her group of friends, it was Suzanne who was the one constantly looking for boyfriend material, and Kate who tried to remind her that bedfriend material was just as good, if not better. Kate always thought it was tough to be in Suzanne's shoes and saw how much she struggled trying to find a man who was not intimidated by her successful career. Another lesson learned from Linda was to avoid falling in love with someone who couldn't (or wouldn't) bring home a paycheck and then held a chip on his shoulder about it. And at age thirty-two, Suzanne was a few years younger than Kate and already felt that she was over the hill for a lot of the men she met. Why should Kate think she should fare any better? "It's not completely up to me," Kate finally answered. "Even if I was looking for a serious, monogamous relationship, it's not like Mr. Right is just sitting around waiting for me. And I'm not about to wring my hands in dire search of him!"

Adam said nothing, just nodded, in agreement with her life approach or merely to show he was listening, Kate wasn't sure. She had come to embrace her lifestyle and to love it, she told herself. She certainly didn't require his approval.

They walked along in silence for a while longer. "I guess I can let go of your arm now," Kate said sheepishly. "No one's around." It had felt sort of nice to walk together like that, Kate admitted. It was … comfortable; she just hadn't wanted *him* to feel awkward, that's all. Had he felt awkward? Did he like playing the part of her fiancé? Kate didn't really want to ask—she needed him now, at least for a little while longer until she got the promotion. Then she could make up some story about the wedding getting called off—that kind of thing happened all the time. She could even still keep her commitment to Alberto and just not tell anyone about the marriage. "Hey, let's grab some dessert," she said to break the silence and lighten the mood. "As long as we're walking this way, we might as well stop for a cupcake."

The line at Magnolia ran outside as usual, composed of a mix of tourists and NY locals. But it was just the right thing to break any awkward tension that tonight's act may have brought between them. Adam may not have completely approved of the way she was going about taking control of her career—he may not have approved *at all*—but for whatever reason, he had come to her rescue tonight. And Kate was happy that they were still close enough friends that they could spend a few minutes standing out on the sidewalk, laughing and licking frosting from their lips. "Remember when your dad made us those red velvet cupcakes?" Adam asked. His eyes lit up at the memory, with a happier expression than he'd had all night.

"He got red food coloring all over the counters!" Kate recalled the blood-like stains that didn't scrub out for days.

"Those were some of the best cupcakes I've ever had," Adam reminisced. "These are a close second," he said, licking frosting from his upper lip. He didn't quite get all of it, and Kate swiped her thumb across his mouth. He turned his head and caught her finger between his teeth playfully and let go quickly when Kate gasped in surprise. It was almost … flirtatious … but the moment was over before Kate could process it. And by the time they had cabbed it home, Kate felt like everything between them was as normal as it had been before.

Things with Kate had taken a turn to everything *but* normal. Adam had not been sure about how he thought this dinner would go, had not thought through the evening past getting dressed and getting there. Winging it all was a very un-Adam thing to do, but this thing with Kate, whatever this thing was, certainly brought out sides of him that he didn't often show.

All of what Adam said about himself was true, though he would never have been so obnoxious about it. He really did vacation in Bali, had a certain preference for private jets when they seemed practical, and during the brief time when he thought he'd take up golfing (Claudia thought it was a good idea), he'd spent it at Pebble Beach. The last several years of hard work and lots of luck in the technology industry had been *very good* to Adam. He knew that the kind of woman that he needed to use his money to impress would not be the one for him. He never imagined he'd use his money to impress a woman's *boss*. At the same time, it was so easy, so natural for them to be a couple. Did she see that? Did she feel how right it was for them to be together?

Adam changed into his sweats and did what he always did to relax in the evening. He opened up his laptop and mindlessly perused the news, Facebook, his email, anything to try to get his mind off of Kate. He had liked seeing her reaction when she first saw him walk into the restaurant. Maybe he couldn't compete with the grungy musician types, but he cleaned up well and he knew it. He didn't really like the Kate that he saw at dinner, though. He could practically see her mentally keeping score against her colleagues. He had met assholes like her boss before, ones who thought fostering a cutthroat environment in the name of "healthy competition" was good for the organization, ones who then proceeded to make irrational decisions based on favoritism and their own egos. Not that he thought promoting Kate would be irrational. Adam really had no idea how good (or bad) she was at her job, though it was hard for him to believe she would be bad at anything she worked so hard at. But it would be irrational for her boss to promote her *now* because he happened to like Adam and the cache that he thought Adam could help bring to the firm. Sure, he'd been impressed by Adam's leisure activities, but he wasn't stupid enough to ignore the fact that Adam sat on several boards of directors and was acquainted with other major names in the Valley. Hell, Adam had already received a LinkedIn request from Kate's boss, which he of course accepted. For Kate.

Adam leaned back against his pillows. This lack of furniture thing was starting to irritate him, but he couldn't hang out at Kate's *all* the time. She had no idea how he felt about her, that much was clear, and annoying her with his constant presence wasn't going to get him anywhere. *You're important to me*, he had said to her. That was the best he could do? He wanted to smack himself in the forehead. Part of him wanted to just tell her, to declare his intentions, so to speak. Or to just grab her and kiss her. But he knew that would just scare her off and that he'd have to be more subtle—to win her over without her realizing it was happening until it was too late, until she'd already fallen for him. He was definitely scoring points with her right now, never mind that it was because she thought Alberto had suddenly changed his mind. He would figure out a way to change her feelings from those of gratitude to—to what? Being attracted to him, wanting him. To go from seeing him as the "safe" boy from her childhood to the grown man he'd become would be a start. Adam yawned and shut down his laptop. The night had gone well, and he had to get some rest to keep up with her tomorrow.

Chapter 10

During their morning run, Adam saw a noticeable change in Kate. She always had good form, but her shoulders were straighter, her stride was the tiniest bit faster, just enough that he could barely keep up. It was worth putting on the show, since it had clearly made her happier. She even smiled at him when they met in the lobby and said "hey" before putting her headphones in.

Kate practically bounced into the office, humming another one of her favorite show tunes, but quickly gathered herself together as she booted up her computer. It wouldn't do to let her coworkers think she was gloating, even though that was exactly what she was doing in her head. And there was an email from the boss, in all caps, all subject with no body text: COME NEXT SAT. YOU AND ADAM.

Clearly she needed to get the details from his assistant, but she had heard some hallway conversation about the annual grill-out at the boss's house in Connecticut. "Yes!" Kate said to herself, grinning widely before schooling her expression in case someone passed by. She settled for singing "Do You Hear the People Sing" from *Les Mis* under her breath in celebration.

Unfortunately the next days at work didn't go so well. The firm had lost investors again, and those that were still with them were anxious. Not as anxious as when the whole Madoff scandal broke or the last major market implosion, but whenever business was bad, the boss became unpredictable at best. He fired an investor relations associate since it was one of her clients that walked that week, and she happened to have just expensed a five hundred dollar dinner on said client. Kate barely escaped one of those late afternoon meetings where the boss went around the table, publicly pointing out all the flaws in each person's work performance. "Emergency meeting in my conference room, Kate," the boss grumbled at her as she headed toward the elevator.

"I'm meeting a client," she responded truthfully.

He narrowed his eyes, as if accusing her of lying, as if any of her actions over the past several years could have led him to question her work ethic.

She gritted her teeth and looked straight into his beady little eyes.

He lowered his head and mumbled something about needing to keep Silicon Valley on the hook. Kate hated that he thought she was ducking out to meet her "fiancé," but she didn't want to run late even if the boss could be argued with. If it weren't for the promotion potential and the paycheck, Kate thought at that moment, she would have been out of that firm years ago.

Money was always a weird subject for Kate, despite it being the central topic of her business school education and career. Kate did not have an uncomfortable upbringing by any means, but all the same, her family only bought things on sale or a generic brand—and this was before Target was *Tarjay*. Linda used to talk about money incessantly—how much getting a pizza delivered was versus cooking at home, how buying books at the book fair was a waste when there was a public library ten minutes away, how much college tuition would be if Kate didn't go to Michigan, where her mother taught. As a result, Kate was aware, *hyperaware* of her personal finances, knew where every dollar of her paycheck went, and appreciated every Louboutin heel that her job afforded her. And she was happy to pick up her half of the restaurant bill on a date or the whole bill if she had been the one to do the asking. Her friends received generous birthday and holiday gifts—whatever amount she needed to spend to get them the item she'd found that was perfect for them. But the best part of her paycheck was that it afforded her the ability to not think about it. She had readily paid off her student loans and never had to carry a balance on a credit card or worry about how to pay for a kid's music lessons—none of the things her mother had had to deal with while her father waited for his "big book deal" to come in.

Kate didn't like to think about money, and she especially didn't like to talk about it. Every once in a while, she would date a guy who tried to impress her with his six-figure salary, who apparently hadn't realized she had a fine six-figure salary herself. But another one of Kate's rules about men—or people in general, really—the phrase "my net worth" should never be spoken in a social setting. So while she had a passing curiosity about Adam's conversation with her boss, it was nothing more than that. She knew he was successful, but so was she. She assumed he had exaggerated a bit, as part of the act he was putting on, and was amused by how heavily her boss had fallen for it. And if the potential of having Adam as a client gave her a break from his assholeishness, she'd take it.

Time with Adam became the saving grace of those couple of weeks. Kate became accustomed to having him come along on her morning run and even had a little fun racing him home on a couple of occasions. And after a bad day at work (and almost every one was bad these days), it was nice to unwind with Adam over a glass of wine and dinner. She even got him to go out to a few restaurants, even though he would have been glad to cook. But after being a guest lecturer for a class in the afternoon and his series of mysterious "meetings" with colleagues in California, she was glad he could enjoy at least some of the culinary offerings Manhattan had to offer.

It was fun for Kate, too, to share some of her favorite places with someone new, someone familiar enough to split an appetizer with or snag a few *frites* from. The staff at the restaurants always assumed they were a couple, and Kate just started to laugh it off rather than try to correct anyone. It was pretty amusing, really, when an older woman, clearly from out of town, walked by their table at Smith & Wollensky and tried to channel Beyoncé when telling Adam that if he liked her, he should "put a ring on it." The woman had even shaken her hand and done a little shimmy. Adam hadn't missed a beat and just said, "Already tried. She won't wear it."

It turned out that they liked a lot of the same food, though he was more of a meat and potatoes kind of guy. There was always something new that Kate would learn about Adam as each day passed, like how he'd met Steve Jobs once, years ago when Adam was first starting out, and how motivated he'd been after that meeting, even though their interaction had been nothing more than a fleeting hello. Kate loved hearing about Adam's teaching, how his eyes lit up when talking about the students who would come up to him after class to talk about some article they'd seen or some new technology they had heard of. "It's so humbling," he said, "to see these freshmen, so articulate about these advanced concepts!" It was nice to see someone so enthusiastic about a job they clearly enjoyed. It reminded her about how Cassandra would go on about her brides and their venues. Kate couldn't remember the last time she'd been excited about her job. Sure, it was nice when the money rolled in, but had it only ever been about the money?

Chapter 11

It was two days before the Connecticut grill-out, and Kate was stressed. Stressed about work (always) and stressed from not having run this morning. It had rained all day, and Kate thought she might have to resort to the treadmill in her building's gym. She left work a little early, to avoid her boss and mostly because she was just in a foul mood.

Kate came home to see Adam jumping up and down in front of her television, apparently playing some video game.

"What. Is. That?" she said loudly, over the sound of crashing and splashing.

"Xbox," Adam called out to her. "Thought it'd be fun." He stopped playing then and turned to her. "Since it's been raining all day and you missed your run, I thought I'd bring it down from my apartment."

"Please don't tell me that you're one of those guys with the headsets who plays all night online."

"My handle is Buttkicker42 … I'm kidding!" he added quickly after she widened her eyes in alarm. "I don't have time for that. These game systems are the future of personal technology."

"So this is an academic exercise?"

Adam grinned. "It's a *fun* exercise. Come on, it's time to get your inner geek on."

Adam waved his arms a few times and turned on some game about dancing.

"What is this?" Kate asked.

"Are you serious? This is a really popular game."

She arched a brow. "I've been too busy living my real life to be concerned about a gaming one."

Adam tsked an amused sigh. "Just get out of that dress and those shoes."

"There's a come-on if I ever heard one," Kate called from her bedroom.

She came back out in a tank top and shorts, and Adam pulled her into position to face the TV. "Just stand here and start dancing when the music comes on."

And in spite of herself and her bad mood, Kate followed the steps of her onscreen character and actually started to enjoy herself. They kept playing until Kate had the moves down enough to start singing along with the music. She also started laughing at Adam.

"You may have smarts, sweetness, and style, but you do *not* have rhythm." He did have enthusiasm though, and as long as Kate steered clear of his swinging arms and legs, she could remain uninjured.

When they finally stopped, Kate grabbed some beer from the fridge and took a long pull from hers as she flopped down on the sofa next to him. She was surprised to find herself out of breath and even sweating a little. She was even more surprised at how much fun she was having. When was the last time she stayed in playing *video games*? That would be never. Linda thought they were frivolous, and well, Kate never played them enough to miss having them.

"You're kind of fun to have around, Ad," she teased, poking him lightly in the ribs, "even though you can't dance for squat!" It reminded her of how they could always count on one another to cheer the other person up, like when he was overstressing about some exam that he was sure to ace or after his brothers had used him as a punching bag again. Or after she'd had to overhear another one of her parents' screaming fights about—what else?—money.

"You're so serious, trying to get every *exact* step." Adam poked her back, tickling her slightly. He imitated her concentrated expression, which was made even funnier by his attempt to blow his hair out of his eyes.

"I'm just trying not to flail my arms wildly like *some* people," Kate laughed. She threw her arms in the air in exaggerated mockery. Adam grabbed her wrists, laughing along with her. The next thing she knew, they were in a tickle fight like two kids, and she laughed harder than she had in ages.

"Damn!" Adam exclaimed, trying to stop a nearly full bottle of beer from toppling behind her. He missed, and they both realized he was practically on top of her, her head back against the arm of the couch, his lips inches from her face. They were both breathless from the dancing, from the tickling. She felt his breath against her mouth, looked into his eyes. His arms were on either side of her—when did he get so … muscular? She'd been in this compromising position a million times before, but never quite like this, and never, absolutely never with Adam. She felt something she couldn't quite describe—the pleasure of having a man in her arms, sure, that was nothing new. But there was something else there, too, more like … joy? She inhaled the hint of her own floral shampoo and soap, combined with his distinctly male scent. She found it almost intoxicating. This feeling, whatever it was, was uncomfortable in its unfamiliarity. *This is crazy.* She could have sworn she felt his erection against her thigh, and her body began to respond in spite of herself. A few inches closer and she could claim his mouth with her own, and her breath quickened at the thought of what he might taste like.

And then what? She could enjoy a passionate evening and go back to friendship as usual in the morning. But what about Adam? She doubted he was the type who had a lot of casual hookups. Not to mention he was just out of a relationship that clearly still held a cloud over his head. But most of all, he was her friend, and the last thing she would do was hurt him. *Don't give him the wrong idea.* She dropped her gaze. "Party foul! At least it's not red wine," she said in a normal tone of voice. Adam moved off of her quickly and smoothly as she moved to clean up the mess. He stood in front of the TV, doing something with the game system, and she was glad his back was turned. Would he have kissed her? Would she have let him? *Yes*. Her answer surprised her, in spite of her still rapid heart rate. "This would just get messy."

Adam turned around then, and Kate realized she said that out loud. "This game," she said hurriedly. "This game could get messy. I don't think I have enough space for it." She still didn't look at him, didn't want to see what she thought she might see. He couldn't, *couldn't* have feelings for her. She needed him, she realized. Not just as a fake fiancé, she needed him as her friend. And he wouldn't be if she broke his heart.

That night after Adam left, Kate was straightening up her apartment, putting clothes into a laundry bag to get taken to the Laundromat in the morning. She went through her mail from the week, had a snack, then wiped up the kitchen a little—all mindless things to keep her occupied, and all things that allowed her thoughts to wander. Two of her best girlfriends were in serious relationships now. And Suzanne was always on the lookout for one, so it would only be a matter of time before she found a boyfriend as well. Kate was happy for them, she genuinely was. But between all their work and dating schedules, there was less and less time for their friendships. And Kate had never been a true social butterfly, even when she could be the life of the party. She'd always valued a few close friendships over lots of superficial ones and had been over the moon that she and Adam had reconnected. She let out a heavy sigh. It was a fine balance for men and women to be true friends. In some ways, it would be simpler, actually, if Adam had a girlfriend. Or even someone to date casually. Kate perked up then. That was it. Adam could relieve all his romantic tensions with someone else, and then the two of them could just be friends.

Kate went to her phone and punched in a text to Suzanne: *I'm setting you up with Adam.*

OK, Kate admitted to herself while she waited for a response—there weren't exactly sparks flying when they first met, but maybe Adam just wasn't the kind of guy to set off sparks right away.

Kate texted again:

Give him a chance. He's nice.

Finally Suzanne responded:

No

One word, that was it? Kate found herself slightly offended on behalf of her childhood friend. Suzanne was normally pretty open to first dates. Kate's fingers flew:

He's smart! He's cute (kind of). He dresses well (sometimes). Funny in a quiet, witty way.

From Suzanne again:

No

WHY???

Date him yourself.

I'm not that kind of girl, Kate responded.

Kate sighed. She knew it was a dead end with Suzanne, and she wouldn't be on a quest to set up Adam and play matchmaker. Even if she did have a ton of single female friends, he was too good for just anyone. She would just have to think of something else.

Chapter 12

After their morning run, Kate gathered up her laundry while still in her running gear. "Best thing about New York is," she said to Adam, "I never have to fold my own clothes, even when I have three weeks' worth of laundry to do!" Adam offered to bring the bags down to the Laundromat for her, but of course she refused, even as she staggered under their weight and bulk. So Adam helped himself to a bottle of water and some breakfast as she left.

A few minutes later, Kate was back, with her full bags and cursing. "The stupid Laundromat is CLOSED. No reason, no idea when it'll be open, no apology, just a sign on the door that says *closed until further notice*. What the fuck is that supposed to mean??"

She really didn't take it well when things didn't go according to plan, Adam thought. He guessed that was part of the disciplined aspect of her personality. She just couldn't understand why other people weren't as regimented. "I'll take care of it," Adam told her.

Kate looked confused again, like she did when he offered to deal with her computer. "The next closest laundry place is a cab ride away …"

"I'll take care of it," Adam repeated, calmly smiling. "I don't have much going on today. Go and get ready for work, and don't worry about it."

Again, she just gave him a puzzled look and headed toward the shower. Adam shook his head. He bet no one had done her laundry since she was twelve and didn't want her dad to see her training bras. Even if he was probably the one who bought them for her.

"You're sure you're OK with this?" Kate asked again as she was gathering her things for work. "You're really going to do all this?"

"There's a perfectly good laundry room downstairs that I'll bet is empty during a weekday. I'll read a book or something."

"This bag is sheets and towels, this one is regular clothes, and this one, umm … this is delicate cycle. If you're OK with that, I mean."

"Kate, I'm thirty-six years old. I've seen women's underwear before."

Kate blushed a little, a pleasant reminder that she wasn't always as cool as she wanted everyone to believe. "OK then, well, I'll see you later. Dinner?"

"Dinner. Now don't be late for work. It'll just make you even more irritable." Adam practically closed the door on her.

"She's still not ready," he said aloud to himself, now that he was alone. He wasn't fooling himself into thinking he could make her fall in love with him by doing her laundry. Her nearly defiant sense of independence made him want to take care of her. Made him want her, period. He almost kissed her last night, and he was pretty sure she wanted to kiss him back. But then something held them both back, and the mood was broken when she practically shoved him away to clean up the beer. He'd nearly cursed out loud then, but he'd always been a patient person. If he made his intentions known too soon, she'd run, she'd emotionally distance herself from him completely. Or maybe he'd become another notch on her bedpost. Either option was unacceptable to him. He wanted it all, he wanted *her* all.

Everything was back to normal, Kate thought as she headed in to work. Adam had greeted her in the lobby at 5:30, they'd gone on their morning run, and there had been nothing at all awkward between them. She hadn't read him wrong last night; she knew he had wanted to kiss her. But he'd obviously realized what a mistake it would have been as soon as she had. He probably still wasn't over Claudia and was in New York to run away from her and their life together. And as for her own reaction, hell, Kate had already admitted Adam was kind of attractive, and she knew herself well enough that it was no surprise she'd be turned on by a guy like him lying on top of her. The exercise from that dancing game had released endorphins in her brain, making her seek out more pleasure, that was all.

All the same, Kate couldn't quite stop wondering what it would have felt like if Adam *had* kissed her. Were his lips as soft as they looked? Would his kiss have started slowly, tentatively, or would he have crushed his mouth against hers like she'd thought of doing to him? Kate inhaled sharply as she wondered what his skin tasted like. *This is ludicrous. This is Adam.* Their almost-kiss was just a rebound move that was narrowly avoided. She should be happy about that. A rebound hookup may be what he needed, but it wouldn't be with her. She would just end up hurting him. Plus, she needed to work with a clear head, without the guilt of anyone's heartbreak on her conscience. And she needed to go to the boss's garden party without any cloud of tension over them.

When Kate got home that evening, she opened the door to the smell of chicken roasting and the sound of a woman's laughter. Her first thought was annoyance—did Adam really bring some woman back to *her* apartment? Was it that brunette from the other night who'd slipped a note in his pocket? But then she realized that she knew that laugh, that it belonged to Cassandra, who she found perched on her kitchen counter with a glass of wine, watching Adam cook. The two of them were nearly doubled over with laughter and Kate found herself in a better mood than before, seeing her close friends get along so well. "What a nice surprise! No brides to manage tonight?"

Cass shrugged. "This one is pretty low-key and didn't want to rehearse. I was in the neighborhood and thought you'd want to grab a bite." She waggled her eyebrows at Kate while Adam was turned away. "But you obviously already have a tasty morsel at home already."

Was there a way to say *shut it* via telepathy? "There's plenty of *food* for everyone. I'm sure Adam's already invited you to stay since that's what *friends* do."

The three of them chatted over a dinner of roast chicken, couscous, and asparagus with plenty of wine to accompany each bite. There was even cheesecake for dessert, which Adam had picked up earlier from one of Kate's favorite bakeries. Cass was telling some of her most entertaining wedding couple stories, and if Adam was at all regretful about the state of his own almost-nuptials, he didn't show it. The two women found a moment to themselves when Adam went to Kate's bedroom to take a phone call. "So it's true," Cassandra said to Kate as soon as Adam closed the door behind him.

"What's true?" Kate asked.

"You're holed up playing house with a gorgeous hunk who is clearly in love with you."

"Stop it!"

"And you're trying to set him up with Suzanne? You've got to be kidding!"

"Did she call you last night?"

"Adam is so into you. Don't tell me you don't see it."

"Adam doesn't read like other men; he's not like that." Kate narrowed her eyes. "Did you come over tonight to see me or to check out Suzanne's theory?"

Cassandra avoided the question, which gave Kate her answer. "When I got here, he was *folding your laundry*. Who does that?!"

"He's just a nice guy."

Cass's eyes widened. "You're into him, too, aren't you?"

"What? No. You've had too much wine, stop being nuts." Kate looked toward the bedroom to make sure Adam hadn't come out and overheard them.

Cass continued, as if having a major revelation, clearly unconcerned about Adam possibly being within earshot. "You haven't been to a party the entire time he's been here. Have you even gone on a date with anyone?" She continued, clearly on a roll. "You come home every night, have dinner in your pajamas, and you're *happy*," she concluded.

Part of Kate wanted to confide in Cass about the near-kiss last night. But saying it out loud would have made it a bigger deal than it was. And it was no big deal, right? "Adam isn't really into going out a lot. It would be rude to do all those things and not spend time with him while he's here."

"When was the last time you *didn't* spend an evening with him?"

Kate drew a blank, but Cass was speedily heading down a path that Kate refused to follow. "I think it's time to say good night, Cass."

Cass laughed. "I do have to be up early tomorrow for wedding prep. But this is so much fun, seeing you fall for someone—"

Kate had had it. She grabbed Cass's jacket and held it out to her.

"Oh, I see," Cass continued. "You want your alone time now, I understand. I won't be the third wheel. Tell Adam I said 'Bye.'"

"Go *home*, Cass."

As Kate was closing the door, Cass propped it back open. "Keep him, Kate. The man can fold a fitted sheet!"

By the time Adam came out to the living room after his phone call, Kate had already cleared up the dishes and was pouring out the last of the wine. When she saw the look on his face, she decided to give him the more generous pour. "Is everything OK?" she asked. Adam just nodded without a word. She gave him his glass and he closed his eyes as he took a big gulp. "Do you want to talk about it?"

"Not much to talk about, really." He didn't meet her gaze. "That was Claudia. I wouldn't normally take a call in the middle of dinner, it's just ..." his voice trailed off.

"It's no big deal, I get it. Exes can be complicated." Kate tried to empathize, *imagining* that the end of a long relationship could be complicated and heart-wrenching. She'd seen enough of what her friends have gone through; she'd just never been in that situation herself. Witnessing it again reminded her of the reasons she kept her love life simple. Simple meant protected.

Adam just stared into his wine, and Kate thought she had never seen anyone so sad. She was reminded of how he looked after his brothers had ganged up on him. *And this is why love sucks.* This Claudia woman must have really done a number on him. After a few minutes, Adam finally said, "I guess we should call it a night" and headed up to his apartment.

The next morning, Kate got a text at 5:30:

Skipping the run.

Chapter 13

Adam found Kate in her bedroom, on all fours, her rear end sticking up from the bottom of her closet. He leaned against the door jamb before feeling guilty for enjoying the view so immensely. "What are you doing?" he asked, to announce his presence. Her response was muffled, something that sounded like *Stop looking at my ass*. Startled, he looked away so she wouldn't see his embarrassment at getting caught. She couldn't have known. "What was that?"

She crawled out of the closet then, her hair disheveled, her cheeks red with warmth. "Stilettos sink in the grass!" she sputtered angrily.

Oh, Adam thought.

"I can't find my wedge espadrilles, and we need to leave in five minutes!"

Apparently there was nothing that flustered Kate like a company social outing, Adam realized. "Calm down. First of all, what is a wedge espadrille exactly?"

She looked at him as if he'd asked what a USB cable was. "It's a sandal with a big heel that looks like straw."

"Go get ready, and I will look for the shoes." Kate gave him another confused look before getting to her feet and going into the bathroom.

Adam looked into her closet—where there was once a neat stack of shoeboxes and rows (and rows) of pristinely lined up heels, there was now a messy pile of shoes without mates. Claudia was never this into shoes, and Kate's collection confounded him.

By the time Kate came out of the bathroom with her hair up and full face of makeup, he had found a pair of matching shoes that looked to him like hay. From Kate's reaction, he knew he'd found the right ones.

"You are so my hero!" she said and blew him a kiss before slipping them on her feet. "Now let's go get this show over with."

On the drive up in the rental car, Kate felt compelled to talk about the elephant in the room. She'd spent a good part of her run trying to figure out what to say to him, to get him to open up to her while still respecting his privacy. "Did you decide to sleep in this morning?" He'd done so much for her, and that was the only thing she could think of to say to show him she cared?

"Yeah," Adam responded casually. He looked directly ahead, his tense jaw and the tapping of his thumb on the steering wheel the only indications of any discomfort he might feel at her question.

Kate took a deep breath. Opening up her own emotions sure wasn't her strong suit. "We're friends, aren't we, Ad?" He glanced at her then, furrowing his brow a bit, as if to say, of course, a ridiculous question. "You can talk to me about her," Kate continued, "you know, if you think it would help."

There was a long pause. It shouldn't be this difficult between them. She supposed time and distance could do this to a friendship, but she wanted to overcome all that, to get back to the comfort they had enjoyed in high school and for most of the time he'd been in New York. "I don't think you'd understand," he finally said.

"Oh," said Kate. *Oh.* Kate had never felt so small. Apparently she wouldn't understand. Why? Because she'd never been engaged before? Never broken up with anyone? *Never been in love before. Oh.* Kate was surprised to find herself blinking back tears. What was it about him that did this to her? She took a few deep breaths, determined to gather her wits about her, letting the hum of road noise stretch between them. She should have known better than to extend an attempt at a deeper friendship than he was interested in. He was doing her a favor because he was just that kind of guy, and when he was through, he'd go back to California and they would just be email buddies again. In another twenty minutes, they would be at the party, and she needed to be on her toes. *Eye on the ball, Kate.*

"So umm, we're thinking about a spring wedding, something small, just family in Ann Arbor," she said softly. She continued to review the bits and pieces of their "story" to be sure they had similar answers to the small talk that would inevitably come up. Adam just nodded every once in a while. Whatever was on his mind, whatever his heartbreak, whatever he thought she couldn't understand about him, she knew he was paying attention and would do this for her. For now at least, that needed to be enough to get her through this day.

Kate had received pseudo invitations to this Connecticut garden party in past years—the type of hallway mention that came along with the disclaimer that "a single city girl probably wouldn't want to spend the day hanging out in suburbia." And the last thing she had wanted was to attend as the lone single person and have people pity her or try to set her up. Or worse, have her boss be in one of his brash moods and ask her what she was doing there—she'd heard that had happened once with one of the lap dogs last year. But this time was different. Her boss's email was as close to a real invitation as she was going to get, and this annual party had become known to be a fantastic networking event with lots of industry people from other firms on the invite list. Attending was all part of Kate's plan to get her career trajectory back on track. Her engagement had become the perfect social excuse to go this year. After all, aren't all married couples supposed to move to Connecticut at some point? And Adam, it turned out, was the perfect prop.

The garden party was not an exceptionally elaborate affair, and the inclusion of children kept it casual. It could have been any backyard grill-out, really, any one that was in a backyard of an acre of manicured lawns, with hired staff to do the cooking and serving, that is. Even the kids had three sitters to oversee the bubble blowing and lawn games.

The search for the missing sandal had made them a little on the late side, but Kate was immediately put at ease as they were introduced to other guests. Her boss might be an asshole, but he was certainly a well-connected one, and since he had taken a liking to Adam, he ushered both of them around the party as if they were his closest friends. Kate was meeting people who worked at other top asset management firms and banks, and there was nothing like an old-fashioned party to get her name out there. She almost felt like she really was the soon-to-be-married rising star at her firm.

By the time Kate was relaxed enough to actually eat something, she found herself at one of the buffet tables with another woman who looked a few years older than she, also wearing a sundress and wedge heel espadrilles. She wore a chunky necklace so intricate that it must have been designer and multiple rings with gemstones the size of gobstoppers. "Jane Koffey," she said, introducing herself. Kate recognized her name immediately, as that of the Managing Director of a new boutique firm that opened just a couple of years ago. It remained to be seen if they would make it or not since the market downturn had been an awful time to be starting up. But Jane was known to be one of the best there was and had been profiled in *New York* magazine as one of the most powerful women in finance. Kate berated herself for not recognizing her. "So you work for that asshole, huh?" Jane said matter-of-factly as she popped an olive into her mouth. "Whoops, I guess I shouldn't insult the host."

"He's a little … rough around the edges," Kate responded diplomatically. She instantly liked Jane, who looked at her conspiratorially.

"I used to be his assistant."

Kate chuckled and was about to ask how one started as an assistant to become MD of their own firm when a small child came running over to where they were standing, holding her hands out in front of her. There was something dripping from them, and Kate tried not to openly look aghast as she stepped back from the child's path, just as the little girl planted her hands on Jane's skirt. "Wipe, Mommy!" the girl was saying.

Jane smiled and let out a sigh as she picked up the little girl. "Chloe, how many times do I have to tell you not to wipe the bubble water on Mommy?"

"Sorry, Mommy."

Jane gave the little girl a kiss on the nose and put her down. Hands now wiped, she ran off back to the other kids as Jane gave a cursory glance at her skirt. "That'll teach me not to wear silk." She made a gesture toward Kate's dress. "I love that dress, almost bought it myself. Make sure to wear it a lot before you have kids!"

"Oh, I don't think I'm going to have kids," Kate responded automatically. She didn't even have to think about what their "story" was. This was the real answer that she had given for as long as she'd been of the age where kids entered in the conversation.

Jane tilted her head at Kate and smiled. "I used to think that, not too long ago, actually." She looked directly at Kate with an expression that was so disarming that, for a moment, Kate was concerned that Jane knew her engagement was a sham. "You can have the job *and* the family, you know. You just need the right support—the right man, the right nanny, the right boss." She looked past Kate over to where the kids were playing. "Looks like you have one out of the three."

Kate turned to where Jane was looking and saw Adam standing with the group of kids. He was waving around some sort of bubble-making contraption and creating a flurry of bubbles, much to the children's delight, if their squeals were any measure. Then one of the boys ran over to Adam and hung on to one of his biceps like a monkey. "You be the tree!" Kate heard the boy yell as Adam swung him around, still holding the bubble-making thing. Adam looked up then and waved at Kate with what looked to be a genuine smile. Kate gave just a small wave back, lest he think to call her over to play with the kids with him. No, she told herself, Adam knew better than that.

Just then Jane's daughter started crying—the high-pitched wail of a child that could only be described as shrieking, and Kate inwardly shuddered. "Sorry, gotta go," Jane said, hurriedly walking to her child. "Drop me a line, we should do lunch in the city," Jane called over her shoulder.

Kate was left alone to watch Adam then. She supposed she really ought to make the best of her time and network with some of the other guests. But she couldn't help but watch him, and how much fun those kids were having, and how he really seemed to be having fun himself. A couple of the other dads seemed glad to leave their kids to play with Adam and be watched by the sitters while they nursed their glasses of beer. *That would be me.* She just didn't have a parental bone in her body.

After a few more minutes, Adam seemed to realize that Kate was not going to brave going through the swarm of kids to reach him, so he made his way toward her. "Sorry, should I be mingling better?" he asked her. "The kids are better company than these blowhards," he grimaced.

"Not everyone's that bad," Kate said, thinking of Jane.

"Maybe so, but trying to impress each other at a fake social event doesn't bring out the best in people."

"What, there aren't any testosterone power plays in Silicon Valley?"

"Touchè. I guess it's just been a while since I've played."

"What is it that you do over there, anyway? All I've ever seen is you sitting in front of a computer." Since they were somewhat alone, Kate wasn't worried about seeming like she knew too little about her own fiancé.

"Nowadays I mostly run an angel investment group and take on an advisory role to some start-ups."

"You're an angel?" Kate smiled. "I guess I'm not the only one you rescue." It made sense. If he was an angel investor, using his own capital to finance new ventures, his conversation with her boss really wasn't such a stretch. In spite of herself, Kate was kind of impressed. Adam was a great catch—for someone out there. Adam seemed to be in a talkative mood, so

Kate took a leap. "So what happened with Claudia? She didn't need rescuing?"

Adam's face clouded a bit, and Kate bit her lip, waiting for him to say something. "The only thing she needs rescuing from is me."

"I don't understand." Was he trying to get back together with her and she was trying to avoid him? She envisioned Adam leaving voicemail after voicemail for Claudia and then finally hearing from her last night. It would make sense that he would be anxious to take her call. And it would make sense that he would be in a bad mood from it if she was trying to blow him off. God, love did crappy things to people.

"We probably shouldn't talk about her now, don't you think? Look happy, or someone's going to think we're having a lovers' quarrel." Adam smiled through his words and reached out to caress her elbow, as if it were the most natural gesture. "We should mingle." He was right, of course, and she followed his lead back to the center of the party, but Kate still felt like he was avoiding the conversation.

Chapter 14

Playing house? Kate's friends thought she was holed up and letting her social life suffer? She fingered the invitation she'd received for a party hosted by *Manhattan Magazine*. It was nice knowing a few people in the entertainment and media industries since finance people weren't exactly known for glamorous fetes thrown around movie releases and magazine covers. This was just the kind of party she and the girls would have swooned to attend while they were in their twenties, and still got a kick out of going to in their thirties. When she'd first received the invitation a few weeks ago, she'd thought she'd decline. But now she thought better of it—it was just the type of New York experience that Adam would never seek out himself, but that he might truly enjoy. Besides, he'd already bought a great suit. Why let it go to waste?

"It's fun to dress up," Kate said to Adam, "to wear something totally outrageous that I'd never get to wear in my regular life." He couldn't seem to understand how it could be that she had nothing in her closet for tonight's party, but still he tagged along on her shopping outing. She was surprised that he'd been willing to come; she thought shopping was most men's idea of torture. "I get to be someone a little different when I go out."

"I kind of like the regular you," he said.

"I'm still regular me, just a more fabulous me." She batted her eyelashes in exaggeration and held up three more dresses for

Adam's opinion. He shook his head at all of them.

Kate scowled. "Men have it so easy. Change a tie, the shirt too if you you're going all out, and *poof*—brand-new outfit."

"But then you wouldn't have excuses to buy clothes you don't need."

"Good point."

"When did you get into fancy clothes? I don't think I ever saw you wear a dress in high school."

Kate shrugged. "I never saw you in a suit before. We didn't even go to prom, did we?"

"What was it that you said about prom? It was for people who didn't realize there was life after high school?"

Kate laughed. "That sounds like high school me. You know I secretly wanted to go, right? I bought a dress and everything. It was a ridiculously poufy thing." She paused for a second. "I thought maybe Harrison Brady would ask me. But he didn't."

"That guy in glee club with you? He was, like, six inches shorter than you." Adam chuckled. "I would have taken you."

"You were only four inches shorter than me," she laughed. "Could you have imagined us at prom? You hate dancing. We would have just spent the entire night sitting and talking."

"Because watching videos in your room was so much better."

"Hey, I was a great prom night hostess! I made microwave popcorn, I got us movies ..."

"The complete collection of John Hughes films is not really a teenage boy's idea of fun."

"You're right, I didn't put out." Kate suddenly felt awkward when her joke was met with silence. It felt odd sometimes that she could feel totally at ease with him, but then suddenly there would be a tension that she couldn't explain.

Kate turned to another rack of clothes and shopped in silence for a few moments. When she turned back to Adam, she saw a perplexed look on his face as he held a dress up and kept turning it back and forth. "Ooohh, that's a nice one!" She grabbed it from him and, indeed, it was the perfect look for tonight. She didn't even have to try it on—her exercise regime ensured that she had remained the same size for years.

"I don't understand which is the front or the back."

He was kind of cute when he was confused, the way his brow furrowed underneath the hair she constantly wanted to brush away from his eyes. "Thanks for finding me a dress!" Kate kissed him on the cheek without thinking, but was startled when he wrapped an arm around her waist and held her there. She took a sharp breath in. Was she giving him the wrong idea? And then he released her just as quickly, as if sensing her discomfort.

"Sorry, thought I was your fiancé for a sec."

Kate smiled brightly. Maybe a little too brightly. "Just for work people. Doesn't need to be all the time."

If Kate's life had gotten a little too blasé over the last few weeks, it definitely was no longer. She'd almost forgotten how much she liked going to parties until she stepped out onto the rooftop at The Peninsula hotel and saw Cate Blanchett posing for a press photo. This was when the Midwestern girl came out in her, the one who was still a little starstruck. The first time she'd been to one of these parties—so many years ago, she wanted to forget how long it had been—she'd almost wanted to ask for a photo or at least an autograph. Thank goodness the friend who'd garnered her the invite berated Kate into appropriate behavior. For a split second, Kate wondered if Adam would be starstruck, but then she smiled to herself. Knowing him, he probably wouldn't recognize a celebrity even if one asked him for computer help.

Kate snagged a glass of champagne from a passing waiter, just in time to find Suzanne, Mia, and Cassandra, who were all enjoying the people watching as much as the celeb spotting.

"Va va voom!" Suzanne exclaimed when she saw her.

"Thank you, darling, I did put in some extra effort tonight. It's been way too long since I've been out, as someone kindly pointed out," Kate responded, directing a nudge at Cass. Adam had found the skin-hugging silver sheath minidress with the low cut back, but she had sweetened up the look with a side Dutch braid that tucked into the nape of her neck.

"Where *is* your fiancé? I thought he was coming with you," Mia said, looking around.

"Not the fiancé tonight, just a friend. He's meeting us here since he might be late."

"Fiancé, friend—I can't keep track," Mia said dryly.

"As long as it's not a work event, I am still on the market," Kate declared.

"And so is he."

"Well, yes, of course. He's not really the type, but sure."

"Maybe you're rubbing off on him."

Mia discreetly pointed to a small group several feet away from them. Adam was at the center of a group of young women, and Kate could have sworn he was writing something on a cocktail napkin. He had apparently said something clever that Kate couldn't hear since the women were twittering with laughter. And once again, Kate noticed the guy really did clean up well. He had combed his hair back again and had kept the perfect amount of stubble along his jaw. He hadn't worn the same suit as the night of the dinner, as Kate had assumed he would. He was dressed in all black tonight, which was a difficult look for most men to pull off. Somehow on Adam, it made him look, well, like a movie star. If he weren't her friend, she might have been tempted to take him home with her.

Adam finally seemed to notice Kate and her friends had arrived and excused himself from his newly formed group of fans. He greeted Mia, Suzanne, and Cass, and then to Kate, he put out a hand to shake. "Adam West, actor. And you are?"

Kate laughed. "An actor, really? And what were you in?"

"You know that movie when the guy meets the girl, doesn't realize she's the one for him, and then he does? I play his best friend. I'm just starting out, you know." The group laughed.

"Those girls bought that?" Suzanne marveled. "Adam West is the actor who played Batman."

"It was the first name that came to me—they're too young to know," Adam shrugged. "One of them asked if I was an actor and I just went with it. I took your advice, Kate, and decided to be someone different tonight. It's kind of fun."

At that moment, a photographer interrupted. "Mr. West, a photo please?"

Kate and the girls didn't know what else to do but to comply, and posed for a group photo with Adam, who acted like he posed for the press all the time. When the photographer was done, Kate couldn't help but burst out laughing.

"What's so funny?" Adam deadpanned. "I could *be* someone someday." He shook his head and held his hand over his chest in mock injury, then left the group to talk to someone else he'd just met.

"He's working the room," Kate said in disbelief, to no one in particular. When did he become so funny? What else didn't she know about him?

Chapter 15

Work had been awful. Again. The boss had been in prime form, yelling so much that Kate had seen spit come out of the corner of his mouth in one of their meetings. One of the lapdogs had even ducked behind a cubicle wall when he'd seen him come around a corner. Kate held her own as usual, cool as a cucumber, head held high. But she'd be lying to herself if she didn't admit that it exhausted her. She was glad for the down time that this walk home afforded her and was really looking forward to going home to Adam this evening. They hadn't talked about going out to dinner, so she tried to guess what he might be cooking. The fresh pappardelle Puttanesca recipe he'd mentioned wanting to try sounded so good, the kind of comfort food perfect for the fall evenings that were getting chillier. She could definitely use some comfort food tonight, along with a little red wine, the chance to put her feet up.

Kate was more than a little disappointed when she entered her apartment and it was dark—no sign of Adam anywhere. When she saw his sneakers lying haphazardly near the door, she remembered he had an evening class tonight. He'd told her right after an extra-long run. They had raced the last few blocks back to her apartment, but she had still been behind schedule and hadn't paid enough attention to what he'd said about tonight. She let out a sigh. It wasn't like she didn't know how to be on her own; she'd done it all this time. It would be nice to catch up with the girls, anyway. She knew Cass has plans with Nick, but Mia and Suzanne were probably around, so she texted them:

Hell day. Bring on the martinis?

Mia texted back first:

So sorry! David just back from work travel. Haven't seen him in a month. Staying in tonight.

Well, who was Kate to stand in the way of love? Or sex.

Suzanne texted back next:

On call. Stop by anyway?

It was nice of Suzanne to offer, but "on call" meant "no drinks." And Kate definitely needed a drink.

She texted Alberto:

Meet for a drink near my place?

Alberto was always fun to have a drink with, and if they felt like something a bit more physical afterward, well that'd be fun, too.

He texted back right away:

Sure

By the time Alberto walked into Kate's favorite cocktail bar a few blocks from her apartment, she was already there at a table for two, already halfway through her first martini. She felt better already, the alcohol taking the edge off her day and the energy from the bar reminding her there was fun to be had. So when she saw Alberto, she offered him a genuine smile. He was just what she needed. He ordered a drink as he slid into the seat next to her.

"I have good news," he said as he kissed her cheeks in greeting.

"Please! I need to hear some after the day I've had."

"Business school might pay off after all. Remember Danielle from our class?"

"Was she the one who got divorced during first year and married during second?"

"That's the one. She's at Sony now and set up a meeting for me for next week. It was good to run into her when I did since she's about to go on maternity leave with her third kid."

It seemed like all the women who had gotten their MRSs

along with their MBAs were now on to babies.

"See, this is why I don't hang out with anyone from B-school," Kate told him. "I don't want to hear about sleep schedules, spit up, and stretch marks." She didn't need to hide her snarkiness from Alberto, knowing he wouldn't think less of her for not wanting what most other women wanted.

"You're a jewel," he said to her as he took her hand and kissed it.

American men just don't know anything about romance. "If only everyone thought so," Kate responded.

"So I take it you had a rough day, then?"

"The boss. You know." Kate didn't want to get into it. She'd vented to Alberto enough times before and didn't want to go back to the foul mood that she had been in just a couple of hours earlier.

"Speaking of the boss, when is that dinner getting rescheduled?"

"What? What are you talking about? I was just going to ask you about why you practically stood me up. Thank goodness Adam was around to pinch hit."

"No, *you* cancelled on *me.* I got your text after I'd spent so long reviewing your notes. I felt like I was studying Black-Scholes all over again. OK, not *quite* like that. But I'll have to prepare again—"

"Wait. I didn't text you." Kate thought back to that day. "I forgot my phone at home. Adam was checking for messages for me, and he said there wasn't anything from you."

They were both silent for a moment. Finally Alberto said, "Adam showed up instead of me? Sounds like he's more than a friend."

By now Kate was fuming. *Who does Adam think he is, messing around with my life? I was getting along just fine without him around, better than fine. He may not approve of how I handle things, but this is my life.* She felt her mouth go dry and her face flush. She'd considered him her closest friend at one time and had been so happy to reconnect. And now he had lied to her. She let so few people into her inner circle, and now she remembered why.

"Sorry, Alberto, I have to … I have to go." Thankfully he seemed to understand. This was what friendship was about—friends let her be and didn't meddle when she didn't want them to. She fumbled around her purse in her fury, trying to find cash to cover her half of the bill.

Alberto covered her hand with his. "I got it," he said gently. Kate just nodded in response, too blurred by her anger to speak. Alberto didn't let go of her hand right away, holding it until she looked at him. "Take care, yeah? Don't be too hard on him. The man must have his reasons."

Kate rushed out of the restaurant and headed toward her apartment, her anger building with every step. Betrayed. She felt betrayed that Adam thought he could come waltzing back into her life after *he* was the one who broke up their friendship in the first place. And then screw around with first her social life (because she hadn't forgotten the guy she might have gone home with at Alberto's last gig), but then to screw with her career? It didn't matter if Adam played the fiancé perfectly. He had lost the right to have any input into her carefully cultivated plans.

By the time she reached her building—*their* building, she thought resentfully—her emotions were about to explode. But she tried to keep to her well-disciplined demeanor. She would give him a chance, she decided, a chance to tell her what he did and why. Maybe he didn't approve of the way she was doing things, but that wasn't his decision to make. She just needed to remind him of that.

She took some deep breaths in the elevator and as she walked down the hall to her apartment. What an end to the worst fucking day, to realize one of her closest friends was messing with her life.

She wasn't surprised to see that Adam was already there when she got home. But tonight she resented the intrusion. She alone determined who came and went from her home, dammit. The brown flip-flops tossed in her entryway were the last straw. Hadn't she told him that New York men don't wear flip-flops?

"Can't you put some socks on or something? I don't really feel like seeing your hairy toes today," she called out.

Adam popped his head out of the kitchen. "Bad day?"

"The worst."

"Do you want to talk about it?"

"No." He went back in the kitchen and Kate could hear him clattering some pot lids or something. Did he always make this much noise? She went into the kitchen. "What are you doing?"

"Steaming salmon and slicing a lemon. I didn't get a chance to eat before class."

"No, I mean, what are you doing here? In New York? In my apartment?" Kate felt heat rising to her face, suddenly needing to know *right now* why he appeared on her doorstep.

Adam wiped his hands on a kitchen towel and tossed it on the counter. Kate grabbed it and folded it over the handle of the oven. *Where it belonged!*

"Are you picking a fight with me?" he asked calmly.

"Maybe." Kate felt her lower lip jutting out like a petulant child before she regained control and tucked it back in.

Adam sighed. "You had a bad day—why don't I make you a drink?" He raised an eyebrow. "Or maybe you've already been drinking? I hadn't taken you for an angry drunk," he said nonchalantly and turned back to the stove.

Was he always this *calm*? It just annoyed her more that he hadn't answered her and was obviously avoiding the conversation. Why did he get to keep his personal life to himself when he knew all her secrets? "I asked you, why are you here? Are things so bad in California that you're running away? What, is Claudia getting married or something? Did you run away because she found a real man?" Kate saw his jaw tense. *Finally, a reaction.* "I told you to put socks on!" she said, unable to think of anything comprehensible.

Adam stalked out of the kitchen. "If I put socks on, will you stop yelling at me for no reason?"

"Tell me why you're here!" she shouted as he went into her bedroom. She saw him putting on his sweaty socks from this morning's run and was satisfied. She was winning. Winning what, exactly, it didn't matter. "You just show up one day and move into my building. And you have nothing to do but hang around my apartment all day? You may not have a life, Adam, but I do. Or I did until you showed up!"

"Don't push me, Kate."

Hah, she thought. *Winning again.* She could figure out how to push his buttons.

"Get your own life, Adam, and stop intruding in mine." She stood in the living room, arms across her chest.

He came back in and stood right in front of her, his arms at his sides, his face inches from hers. It annoyed her more, how tall he'd gotten, how he seemed to tower over her now. His eyes blazed a deeper shade of blue than she'd ever seen before. He spoke in a low, angry tone at first, one she had never heard before. "You said you were getting married," he said slowly. "On Facebook," he added with disgust. "I wanted to give you the benefit of the doubt. I wanted to see if you'd found a real relationship, a real partner." He stepped back from her. "But no, I came out here and found a sham. Planning your way to city hall with a guy you're not remotely in love with, wearing a fucking piece of glass on your finger, playing games at work to get ahead." His eyes flashed and his speech quickened with annoyance. "When are you going to grow up, Kate? You wonder why you haven't been promoted in five years? You can't handle the responsibility. You're even sleeping with the same guys you did when we were in college. Play an instrument or at least pretend to? Check. Don't own a tie? Check. Can't commit to anything beyond three hours from now? Check." He stepped closer to her again, so she could feel his breath on her face and she had to turn away slightly to avoid seeing the disappointment in his eyes. "You're afraid, Kate. Afraid to be an adult, to have an adult relationship because you're afraid to get hurt."

Kate was hot with anger and fighting back tears, thankful that she'd already tilted her face from his. No one had ever spoken to her this way. She would not give him the satisfaction of crying in front of him. She cried in front of no one.

"Get out," she whispered. He didn't move. "You're just envious," she said, even though that statement rang hollow. "You wish you could be me, with my freedom. You don't have the balls to get out there like I do. You're just jealous because you don't have fun like I do." She was on a roll now and turned to glare at him. "You can't even bring yourself to call that girl from the bar who was hitting on you. You're just the same nerdy kid you always were." Adam's jaw tensed again. He clenched his fist as he moved toward the door, the only show of any emotion. How could he be so in control while causing her to lose any sense of it? She suddenly recalled one of his high school science projects, when he built a robot—his "experiment with artificial intelligence" he called it. "You're such a—robot," she goaded him. "A jealous robot." She knew this made no sense at all. How was it that he'd brought out an entirely non-sensible, emotional side of her?

"Maybe I am jealous," he said tersely. "But not for the reasons you think."

"I know you lied about Alberto cancelling. You had no right."

Adam's expression softened then, and to Kate's satisfaction, he looked guilty. "I didn't, I know." He seemed at a loss for words, which fueled her anger. She held such careful control over her life, and he was thoughtless about meddling with it.

"Why did you do it?" she spat out.

"I just … I wanted … I wanted you to see—"

"What? You wanted what? To get a taste of what my life is like? You're that petty? You need to go," she said, opening the door.

He faced her again, but she couldn't look at him. Let him think that she was merely angry, without letting him see the hurt that she knew was in her eyes. "One day, Kate, you'll find someone who loves you for everything you are. And not just the façade you put on. Beautiful." She flinched. "Smart. Vibrant. Insecure." She was surprised at that last one and looked up at him. His expression was tender and then turned to steel again. "Don't miss out on him because you're stubborn."

For a moment, she wanted to just tell him she was sorry for everything she'd just said, but she'd learned over the years how to use her wounds to her advantage, to use them as a fire that lit her determination, her ambition. And tonight she found it was a fine line between hurt and anger. *He* was the one who lied about Alberto cancelling. And now she was so angry she didn't care why he did it, just that he had no right to intrude on her life like that.

"You're a jerk," she said reflexively, knowing as soon as she said it that she didn't mean it.

"I'm not here to be your doormat or your punching bag. Or your prop for whatever show you think you're putting on." His voice was low and angry again, as if he could barely contain his emotions. She'd never seen him angry before. "Go and marry your fuck buddy, Kate. I'm not always going to be here to stop you from sabotaging your own happiness." She felt herself flush, but she said nothing, just stared at his back, at him carrying his ridiculous flip-flops while he walked down the hall in his socks. He didn't turn around, didn't even toss her a sideways glance when he turned the corner. Finally she closed the door and leaned against it, letting the metal cool down her anger. And when she eventually caught her breath, she sank to the floor and sobbed.

Chapter 16

The next morning, Kate was back in control. Her eyes were a tad puffy, but nothing that wouldn't go away by the time she got in to work. She had already resolved to apologize to Adam when she saw him for their run, so she dressed quickly and went to the lobby. When he wasn't already there waiting for her, she checked her watch. 5:29. The doorman at the front desk shrugged his shoulders when she looked his way. It wasn't like him at all, so she waited until 5:35 before heading out by herself.

The crisp, fall air and quiet morning energy of a city about to wake up did its usual job of relaxing Kate. But she missed Adam, she realized, missed knowing that he was right behind her. She had missed her friend, after all these years of being just fine on her own and making new friends, she missed the one person who knew all the facets of her personality, who had shared their own history together, who apparently knew her better than she knew herself. It took willpower not to cut her run short. When Adam was there, the time flew by. Today she just wanted to run back to their building and find him, wake him up to tell him she was sorry for picking a fight, that she didn't mean what she had said. That he had clearly grown up and out of the insecurities that she herself was still fighting.

Finally, after she got in her full hour, she went to her apartment and saw that Adam hadn't been there. *He must still be really mad*, she thought. She showered with her phone on the bathroom sink, in case he called or sent a text. Finally she decided to call him herself—she was the one who needed to do the apologizing, after all. But when she went to call him, she realized she had an email from him, that he had written early in the morning, before the run. She felt even worse realizing that he had emailed instead of texted so that he wouldn't wake her.

"I'm sorry for how I left things, I shouldn't have said the things I did. Going back to CA today. I'll ping you later."

Kate felt a lump rise in her throat as she dialed him. The call routed to voicemail, and she hung up. *He's gone.* She had always hated when she and Adam argued back when they were teenagers. This brought back those memories and something more. This felt different. She didn't feel certain that they would make up. She looked at his message again. *I'll ping you later.* Was that like "I'll call you" after a one-night stand? He didn't say if he was coming back, and even if he did, would it just be to pack up his things for good? She must have really pissed him off for him to just *take off* like that, literally in the middle of the night. She didn't blame him, really. He obviously had a life in California, so why shouldn't he go back when his only friend in the city just chewed him out for no reason?

Kate gave herself another minute to sit on the edge of her bed, trying to take deep and steady breaths. "Get a hold of yourself," she said out loud. It might be hours before Adam was reachable by phone again if he'd gotten an early morning flight. She needed to get herself to work and focus on the day ahead. No use sitting here sulking over a fight with a friend. *A friend,* she repeated to herself.

All the same, Kate found herself unable to concentrate all morning, taking more trips to the water cooler and coffee machine than she needed to, just to keep herself from sitting at her desk watching the minutes pass. Finally, after drinking way too much caffeine, she typed out a message to her girls, wanting some advice from any or all three. It was so unlike her, to be the one needing support and input about a guy—a guy who was just a friend, no less. She summarized the fight, how she found out he lied about Alberto not being able to show up to the dinner. She slowly typed out that she was upset about it all. *I miss him.* She looked at those words again and couldn't believe she typed that. She deleted that line. And then typed it again. *I miss him being around,* she added. Then deleted those last two words. *I miss him.* She stared at those three words again and left them there. She could admit this to her closest friends. She exhaled and hit send before she could talk herself out of it.

Suzanne wrote back first:

I'm sorry you're upset. Maybe this is what it took to realize you're in love.

Kate just stared at that message for a few moments. And repeated the last few words to herself over and over. *You're in love. You're in love.* Was that what this was? This ache she felt? This couldn't be. Love wasn't supposed to make you feel like crap. Not at first, anyway. And they'd never even been a couple. How could she have fallen for someone if they'd never even been together?

But she hadn't felt like crap before last night. All the fun they had together, how being with him was the best part of her day—had they been dating and she hadn't even known it?

More messages came in, from Cassandra and Mia, both echoing Suzanne's assessment. Kate hit reply all:

Do you think he's going to come back?

Kate hit the refresh button repeatedly, waiting for their answers.

Cassandra was the first to reply:

He's been trying to win you over for weeks. Maybe you need to reciprocate.

Suzanne followed shortly after:

He's been pretty patient. It's your move.

Kate sat back in her chair then and thought about all the things Adam had done for her since he arrived. It almost made her sick to her stomach, thinking how she had started taking him for granted, how she had come to almost resent his presence. Now she wanted nothing more than to see him. It wouldn't be enough to just talk to him on the phone, she decided. If she loved him, if she really did love him, and she wasn't exactly sure, then she needed to see him to know. And she needed to see him to know if he loved her back.

She clicked onto a travel website. She wasn't going to do anything rash. It couldn't hurt just to see what the schedules were like, she told herself. Her heart started beating faster when she saw there was a nonstop flight to San Francisco from LaGuardia. She'd have to drive an hour down to Palo Alto, but if she left now, she could make the flight. Her mouth felt dry, and she felt the heat rise to her face with anticipation. She was really going to do this? She took a glance at her calendar. There wasn't anything scheduled that she couldn't change. In a few clicks, her ticket was purchased—one way, no less. She'd figure everything out once she got there. Once she'd seen him, they would figure out the rest.

She started gathering her purse and buzzed her assistant. "I'm not feeling well. Cancel all my meetings for the rest of the day." She paused and then said, "Tomorrow too." It was true, Kate justified to herself. She did feel sick to her stomach.

There wasn't any time for Kate to stop at home, so she grabbed a cab and headed straight to the airport. She kept checking her phone, but still no word from Adam. As she boarded the flight, she sent one last message to her girlfriends. *On way to Palo Alto. Wish me luck.*

Chapter 17

Kate had barely slept during the long flight. She could only replay, over and over in her mind, every evening she had spent with Adam. Had she mistaken their chemistry together for a long-term friendship? Then she remembered the night he had almost kissed her. Or she had almost kissed him. There was no mistaking the attraction at that moment, but she had misinterpreted it as solely physical, without any of the emotion she was feeling now. So here she was, in a rental car, behind the wheel for the first time in years, driving south on Route 101 to the last physical address she had for him. She had decided on the plane that she wouldn't call him when she landed, that after coming all this way, she needed to see a genuine reaction when he saw her, not a reaction he could prepare for. She assumed that would tell her where they stood, that she would know her own feelings once she saw his.

There was a certain type of person that the West Coast was suited for, and Kate was not it. Too much driving, too much sun, too much color. She had taken off her black blazer, but was still in her black shift dress, as she cursed the bright California sunshine streaming through the windows. She now understood why no one wore black here, as she started to sweat in sixty-five degree weather. She didn't even want to think about what driving was doing to her heels. She caught her reflection in the rearview mirror and frowned, realizing she had no hairbrush, no makeup, nothing to freshen up with before she saw him. No matter, she told herself, he'd seen her look worse. She pressed on the accelerator, feeling like she couldn't get to Palo Alto fast enough.

Kate's confidence started to lower when she realized the GPS directions were taking her toward beautiful tree-lined streets of large single-family homes with perfectly manicured lawns. The address she had must have been for the house he shared with Claudia. A few more turns and she would be there, at the house of his ex-fiancée, the woman who quite possibly had broken his heart not too long ago. Kate took a few deep breaths and kept driving. There was no turning back now, not after she had travelled so far. If Claudia was there, she would just introduce herself as an old friend of Adam's, that's all, and ask if she had his address. She could say she happened to be in town … or something. She tried to convince herself that Claudia would even be happy that some other woman was looking for Adam after she herself had discarded him. But she knew women well enough that they never enjoyed seeing an ex with someone else, no matter the circumstances. Even Linda made snide remarks about women her father was seen with around town.

The GPS announced that she had arrived at her destination, and Kate looked up to match the address to the beautiful, no, *gorgeous* house that she'd pulled up in front of. It looked newly built, with potted flowers on the porch and lights on inside that made it warm and inviting. The opposite of where she lived. There was even a palm tree on the lawn. *A fucking palm tree*. She was willing to bet there was a pool in the back, too. It all made sense, of course, since a warm home was all Adam had ever wanted while growing up.

Kate parked and let out one last groan of dread. She got out of the car and smoothed her dress with her palms, trying not to look like she just spent the past seven hours sitting in cramped spaces. She ran her fingers through her hair as she walked up the stone pathway, catching herself as one of her narrow heels wobbled along a stone edge. She didn't even have the right shoes for this, she thought, as she rang the doorbell nervously.

Claudia was petite and brunette, with a short bob, wearing a periwinkle V-neck T-shirt and faded blue jeans. She was—cute. Nerdy, but cute. She was *exactly* what Kate would have imagined Adam's fiancée to look like, if Kate had allowed her mind to wander that far. Kate felt ridiculous, standing on this woman's doorstep, dressed as she was, and her words come out rushed and jumbled. She barely heard herself saying something like, "Looking for Adam … the only address I have … d'you know where he is?"

Claudia's expression was confused—and no wonder; it wasn't every day some Amazon woman showed up at your doorstep looking for your ex-fiancé. She called out behind her. "Ad? There's someone here to see you." Kate felt beads of perspiration form on her forehead that had nothing to do with the California sun. Oh my God, Adam is *here*? The call from Claudia the other night, his sudden departure. They must be reconciling. "Would you like to come in?" Kate realized Claudia was speaking to her and holding the door open wider.

"N-no," Kate stammered. Before she could think of anything else to say, Adam was at the door. Standing with Claudia in the entryway of *their* home, they looked like they belonged together, matching faded jeans and all. Kate instinctively took a few steps backward, as if she could run back to the car and pretend she'd never rung their doorbell.

"Kate," Adam said, clearly surprised, but not clearly pleased, the way Kate had envisioned their meeting. "What are you doing here?"

"This is *Kate*?" said Claudia, suddenly showing more anger than confusion. She crossed her arms over her chest and her eyes narrowed at Kate.

The way Claudia was looking her up and down triggered Kate's defenses. "The one and only," Kate responded with confidence she didn't feel.

Adam stepped down to the path in front of Kate, still in his bare feet. "You flew here to find me?" he asked. But Kate couldn't stop looking at Claudia, how perfect she looked for Adam.

"This was a mistake," Kate said softly. It came out as barely more than a whisper, but she knew Adam heard her as she turned to walk back toward the car, trying not to wobble from her nerves.

Adam started following her and she heard Claudia say, "As if the neighbors don't have enough to gossip about." Kate felt the back of her neck bristle then. Claudia resented this little intrusion on their idyllic suburban life, did she? Well, she may have won Adam, but Kate didn't have to lose this battle lying down. She stopped and squared her shoulders and put on her best Bitchy New Yorker. She turned to Adam then, bewildered, *handsome* Adam, and kissed him on the mouth, hard and intending to be fast. But she held him there long enough for her to taste his lips and feel how soft they were, long enough to enjoy the feel of his tongue against hers. He responded, too— how could he not? She was used to men turning to putty in her arms. That had been her intention, hadn't it? Let him see what he would miss? What she wasn't used to was the torture it was to tear herself away from him, wanting to lose herself in these arms that had wrapped around her waist. She let herself enjoy him for a moment, to satisfy her curiosity about what he tasted like. Strawberries. Fresh-picked. She let herself pretend this was the kiss she'd flown across the country for, that he'd picked those strawberries for her and had snagged a few before she arrived. Her eyes stayed shut and her lips lingered against his, knowing it could be the last moment she had with him. She finally pulled away, with every ounce of self-control she could muster, knowing he wasn't hers, was never hers.

She forced herself not to look at him, didn't want to see his sympathy or pity. She looked directly at Claudia, satisfied to see the perfect little woman's mouth agape. "I'm done. He's all yours." She climbed into the car and started the engine, even as she heard Adam asking her to wait.

Kate drove for nearly ten minutes before she pulled over, checking the rearview mirror even though she knew Adam couldn't possibly have chased her down in his bare feet. That is, if he had even wanted to come after her. It was almost déjà vu, just like the last time she'd come to see him in Palo Alto, when they were freshmen in college. Only this time it was worse. Back then, they'd just been friends who had had a falling-out. Now? They were—what? Still just friends, and maybe not even that anymore.

She put her head against the steering wheel and tried to catch her breath. She'd gotten it all wrong. He hadn't been falling for her after all. That night when he'd almost kissed her, it had just been a moment of weakness for him, a diversion from the real relationship that he'd been trying to get back to with Claudia. She squeezed her eyes shut and tried not to imagine them going back inside their cozy little house together, curled up on a comfy sofa, laughing at her. Poor Kate, who had dropped everything to fly all this way. Because she thought she had a chance with Adam? She thought she could break up their happy little home here in paradise? She had a childhood history with Adam, sure. But he and Claudia had romantic history, and years of it. They had—correction, *have*—a life together. She was shaking with humiliation, but even more, she was shaking from the heartbreak.

After a few minutes, Kate was composed enough to drive again, but she knew she wouldn't make it all the way to San Francisco like this. So she decided to go to the closer San Jose airport, the very same one that he had dropped her off at all those years ago, the last time they had truly been friends.

The flight choices were slim, and none of them would take her directly home. Kate decided on one that went through Minneapolis, with a flight to New York in the morning. It wasn't ideal, but at least she knew someone in Minneapolis, and most of all, it got her out of California *now*.

As Kate sat at the gate to wait to board her flight, she felt composed, in control once again. She called Elizabeth and told her she would be in town, and as expected, Elizabeth told her that she'd pick her up from the airport, that she'd love to have her.

Chapter 18

One of the things Kate had always loved about Elizabeth was her ability to take life at face value. And it was the same this evening when Elizabeth picked her. If she had noticed anything amiss about the situation, like the last-minute nature of this visit or the fact that Kate had no bags and only a purse, she didn't let on. Kate offered an apology for the sudden drop-in, to which Elizabeth only replied, "Are you kidding? I got to come to the airport *all by myself* while Matt's with the kids. I'd say we should stop for a manicure, but of course your nails are already immaculate!" Too bad her nails were just about the only thing about her that didn't look worse for wear. She was completely exhausted and looked it. But slinking into the passenger seat of Elizabeth's minivan during the ride to Elizabeth and Matt's house, Kate already started to feel a bit better.

When they arrived at the house, a beautiful five-bedroom brick colonial that was the model of suburban swank, Kate immediately found herself in the middle of a small storm of kids. To Kate, kids fell into one of three age groups. Baby— wore diapers, often needed to be carried. Big Kid—not yet a dreadful teenager, old enough to self-entertain with some sort of handheld video game device. Little Kid—something in between Baby and Big. Elizabeth had one of each, all of whom had surrounded her, clamoring over one another to be heard. Big Kid was complaining that Little Kid got fingerprints on her Nintendo screen, Little Kid was saying Big Kid wasn't sharing, and Baby was clad only in a diaper as she pulled on Elizabeth's pants with a cry.

Elizabeth looked down at Baby and then at Kate. "You'd think after three kids, Matt would have learned how to dress them by now." Kate just smiled. Even with the sarcasm she knew Elizabeth adored Matt and gave him a lot of credit for being as involved with the kids as his work allowed. And, of course, Matt came out to greet them just then, carrying baby clothes and wearing a pirate hat. He said hello to Kate with a kiss on the cheek and then cried "Ahoy, maties!" as he scooped up Little Kid in one arm and Baby in the other. Big Kid was told to get her homework done before bedtime.

Kate was left alone in the family room for a bit while Elizabeth and Matt got the kids settled in for the night. Two of the kids, anyway. Little Kid wearing Cookie Monster pajamas and one sock came over to where Kate was sitting on the couch. He stared at her for a moment, sipping a straw cup filled with milk in one hand and holding a hardcover picture book in the other. He awkwardly, but determinedly, climbed onto Kate's lap. She was so startled that she just sat there. She didn't help him up, but at least she didn't push him away, as was her first instinct. He tapped the book with his index finger. "Read it," he said and then snuggled in to lean back on her, still drinking his milk. Kate was at a loss, having never read a child a book before. So she did as she'd been instructed and read the book about dinosaurs. *This isn't soooo bad*, she thought, but she was somewhat relieved to reach the end.

"Read it again," Little Kid said, still not removing his mouth from his straw or even turning to look at her.

"Uhh, OK," Kate responded. At the end of the story, Kate looked up and saw Elizabeth watching them from the stairs.

"OK, Justin," Elizabeth said. "Story's done, now go up to bed."

Little Kid turned to Kate then and stared at her, as if trying to decide on something. Kate thought to herself that she'd never seen eyelashes that long or eyes so wide. She was suddenly worried that she'd disappointed him somehow. Should she have done goofy voices for him? He took his bottle out of his mouth and hugged her. She didn't know what else to do other than hug back. Had she ever hugged anyone so tiny before? His little bones felt so fragile. She hoped she wasn't squeezing him too hard because she suddenly realized that she needed this hug, had probably needed a hug for a while. She blinked back a tear, glad that Elizabeth was too far away to see her do it, glad that her face was behind his soft, curly hair that smelled like baby shampoo. "Thank you," he said cheerily and tucked his straw back in his mouth as he hopped off the couch with his book.

"You're welcome," Kate whispered, but he was already halfway up the stairs by the time she'd found her voice.

"Sorry, Kate," Elizabeth said. "One more thing, and I'll be right back down."

"No problem," Kate responded, glad that she was able to muster a normal tone. She was glad to be alone for a few more moments, to gather herself together. It had been a while since she had done the math, since Kate had long decided or convinced herself that it wasn't necessary. Growing up, she had originally thought the math would work like this for her: *Date in college, married by twenty-four, kid one by twenty-six, kid two by twenty-eight, kid three at thirty*, with a career somehow along the way. While in college, she thought she would leave a little more time for establishing a job and playing the field: *Date two years, married by twenty-eight, kid one by thirty, kid two by thirty-three*. By the time she had hit twenty-eight, she was a rising star at her firm, and there wasn't any *one* man she was particularly interested in. So she had decided she probably wouldn't get married, that she didn't want to get married. And since then, every time she heard about a heartbreaking divorce like Suzanne's, she congratulated herself on making the right choice. What would the math be now? She didn't allow herself to do the calculations. The arrangement with Alberto aside, she didn't even have a man remotely in the picture, not with Adam gone.

When Elizabeth came back downstairs again, the two women were left alone to catch up over glasses of wine and a plate of cheese and crackers. "Mmmm, miracle mommy juice," Elizabeth sighed contentedly after taking a big sip from her glass. Kate just chuckled and took another big hunk of Brie to spread on her cracker. She hadn't realized how hungry she was until just now and continued to just eat for a few moments until Elizabeth finally said, "So. What are you doing here?"

Kate wasn't the least bit offended by the directness. They had already caught up on the niceties of how happy they were to see each other in the car. She had just been waiting, really, for a good time to tell Elizabeth about the fake engagement, the past few weeks with Adam, and this horrible day. Had it really just been one day since she set out on this cross-country chase after Adam? And now it was quiet in the house, Matt was on kidwatch, and they had enough wine to make the words come easier.

Elizabeth mostly just nodded as Kate spoke, asking clarifying questions here or there or reiterating what Kate had just said, partly to make sure she'd heard it right, partly to make Kate say it and hear it again. Kate expected Elizabeth to be a bit more shocked, but she merely said, "Well, things sure are different in suburbia."

And as Kate heard herself retell her story, she heard it for what it was. Love found and love lost, all in a single day. She placed her hands at her temples and leaned her head forward. "Unbelievable, right?"

Elizabeth offered a tight smile. "It was bound to happen to you sometime."

"Heartbreak?"

"Love."

"This sucks if this is what love is. I can't even describe it. It just—sucks."

"It doesn't have to."

"I'm sorry, I didn't mean it sucks for everyone." Kate tried to remember her manners. "It clearly works for you."

"Matt and I have more than love. We want the same things, and well, we had good timing and luck." Kate just furrowed her brow, clearly new at this and needing more explanation. "We were both single and open to having a relationship at the same time. It gets harder once other people come into the picture. I didn't even have a job yet when we got married, so it was an easy decision for me to go wherever Matt was going to be for med school. And when I got pregnant, well, it made sense to be near his family. From the time we were dating, we built our lives together. It gets harder when each person already has their own life."

"It gets harder as you get older, you mean." There it was again, the unrelenting sound of the biological clock that had been rearing its head recently. Kate knew Elizabeth didn't mean to be insulting, and she actually appreciated having someone to speak so openly with, especially since she was so far from her girls at home. It still didn't feel right, though, to have figured out who she was, built a life—all on her own—and then when she'd wizened up about whom she wanted to share it with, poof, he was gone.

"It gets harder when you have your own lives, yours in New York, his in California. If he's back with his fiancée now, it'd be hard to take him away from everything." Elizabeth lightened her tone a bit. "Even with those legs of yours." Kate smiled. Elizabeth knew her well enough to know that she didn't want a pity party, and she could hardly mourn a relationship that she hadn't even really had.

"You make it sound like you gave up everything for Matt. But you're obviously happy."

Elizabeth shrugged. "I was twenty-two when we got married. I didn't have much to give up! We built our lives together. None of our decisions—his school, giving up a job I loved—none of it was made by just one of us. But yeah, I've never been happier. Constantly exhausted, but happy."

"Do you miss it? The job, I mean."

"Sometimes. Being a buyer for a major department store chain can be a lot of fun. It's a different kind of energy, and I sometimes miss getting dressed for work, seeing coworkers, talking about something other than the kids." Elizabeth chuckled. "And I *really* miss being able to go to the bathroom without interruption!"

It hadn't been an easy decision for Elizabeth to quit her job three years ago. Kate remembered how torn she was back then, but the reality was that she was missing so many days of work due to their son's asthma that she had felt like she was doing a poor job of being a mom *and* a poor job of being a buyer.

"The thing is," Elizabeth continued, "having it all is a myth. Something's gotta give. Even if I had stayed at my job, I never would have risen in my career like you—I just wouldn't have been able to put in the hours or the travel necessary since someone still would have had to relieve the nanny." She shrugged a little. "Matt put in so many years of training to become a doctor, so it was pretty easy to see that I'd be the one staying home. I'm sure the decision would have been harder if I'd had a serious career of my own already."

Kate had heard other women talk about how hard it was to juggle family and career, but had never thought about it applying to herself. It was always something she thought were their own problems that they brought upon themselves. Harsh, perhaps, because she hadn't thought about why they were in the position they were in, that falling in love had brought them there. "So maybe it's not so bad, that this *thing*, whatever you want to call it, with Adam isn't going to work out." Kate felt Elizabeth looking at her, studying her expression as she tried to keep her demeanor neutral.

"If that makes you feel better," Elizabeth finally said.

"It's simpler anyway, to just focus on my job, and date around when I feel like it. No one's feelings get hurt." *Especially mine.*

"If that makes you feel better," Elizabeth repeated.

Kate swallowed some more wine. "It does."

That night, as Kate lay in the guest bedroom, wearing a set of borrowed pajamas from Elizabeth, she stared at the ceiling, knowing that she would get back to her "real life" tomorrow. A life without this hare-brained scheme to be with Adam. This was completely out of character for her. *She* was the one who was romanced, who was wined and dined, who received flower deliveries every other week, who was once serenaded by a man wearing nothing but a guitar. She was not the one who did the chasing. And yet she had just chased a man across the country. Everyone was entitled to a little brain freeze, she told herself. That was all this was—a brief lapse in judgment. She took several deep breaths—it was time to get back in control of her life, in control of her emotions. She mentally listed the things she needed to take care of at work, tasks she irresponsibly left up in the air today. Satisfied with her next course of action, which was merely to get everything back to as normal as possible, Kate let exhaustion claim her and fell into a sound sleep.

Chapter 19

The cramped seats of an economy class ticket, the drone of the engines, the sounds of muffled coughs of strangers shifting in their seats—they had become all too familiar to Kate these past two days. She hadn't minded flying before, but was grateful that she was on the last leg of her trip, on the final descent into LaGuardia Airport. She still couldn't believe what had happened and was trying not to dwell on how *wrong* it had all turned out. A grand romantic gesture that had exploded in her face. Even sitting next to complete strangers, Kate couldn't help but feel herself flush with the humiliation as she envisioned the two of them, Adam and Claudia, standing in the threshold of their perfect little house. *Get a hold of yourself.*

The plane finally landed, and Kate performed the comfortingly familiar task of hailing a cab to get a ride to her apartment. As they drove through Manhattan, Kate's spirits rose and she began to feel more like herself. *Home.* She told herself that the weight in her chest was merely from the travel. Who wouldn't be exhausted after all these flights across the country?

She was already late to work, but she needed to go home to shower, change her clothes, put up her hair. She couldn't imagine what the gossip would be if she went into the office wearing yesterday's outfit, rumpled no less, doing the walk of shame like a twenty-two-year-old. Worse, the gossip wouldn't even be true. In spite of it all, Kate laughed a little, thinking of the *fun* times she'd had when she'd gone home the next morning in a crumpled dress.

A text came in from Cassandra:
Well?
Kate texted back:
Almost home. Alone.
Are you OK?
I will be.

She meant it, too. Kate greeted her doorman with a big smile on her way to the elevator. Her life was her own again, without Adam around to entertain. She had a party coming up that was sure to be filled with attractive single men.

She opened her door, eager to get into the shower and find herself again beneath the grime of travel and the moment of idiocy that brought it upon her. "What was I thinking?" she said aloud as she slipped off her shoes.

"What *were* you thinking?" came the soft response.

Kate nearly jumped out of her skin as she walked over to the couch, where Adam was lying down, arms behind his head as if he'd fallen asleep waiting for her. He got up and closed the space between them, standing close enough for her to smell the clean scent of shaving cream and shampoo. *Her shampoo, actually.* His proximity was unnerving, and she instinctively took a step back.

But Adam just stepped forward again. "You went to Palo Alto to find me," he said gently. "What were you doing?" Kate kept backing up, and Adam kept stepping forward, until her back was literally against a wall. He leaned in closer to her, resting one arm behind her head, with the other hand casually tucked into his front pocket. She could feel his breath on her cheek, and her own breath quickened in response. If she just raised her face a tiny bit, she could kiss those lips again and get another taste of him—for pleasure this time, instead of jealousy. "What were you thinking," he said again slowly, "when you came to find me?" He smiled a little, clearly just wanting her to say it.

Say what, exactly? That she missed him? That she ran cold when she thought about him turning his back on her as he left her apartment? That she hadn't imagined how warm her life could be until she came home to him every evening? That eating ice cream from the carton with him was more fun than picking at a soufflé at a fancy restaurant with her man of the week? "I think …" she began slowly.

"Yes?" He picked up a lock of her hair and twirled it between his fingers. It was an innocent gesture, imitating the habit she'd had since she was a kid. Yet the way he was looking at her, the way he was caressing that lock of curl between his fingers, was more sensual than if he'd been undressing her already. He moistened his lips as if to say something, but then stopped, still waiting for her.

"I think," she whispered, "you'd better kiss me now." He leaned in slowly, brushing his lips across hers, barely touching them at first. She was just thinking that she couldn't bear any more teasing when he kissed her—a real kiss that was soft, yet powerful as a drug. If not for the wall against her back, Kate felt as though she might have fallen to the floor, she was so weak in the knees. She felt the muscles in his back, so familiar, and yet … not. She ran her hands through his hair—how many times had she wanted to brush it out of his eyes?

When they finally paused to catch a breath, Adam said, "So is that what you came to Palo Alto for?"

"Maybe," she teased.

"Or was it this?" He kissed her hard, taking her mouth with his, pressing his body against hers. He kissed her until her lips were raw, then trailed his tongue along her neck, as if wanting to taste every inch of her.

"Bedroom," she gasped.

He paused to say "No," then continued to kiss her neck, a little more gently now, a little less urgently.

"Wha—what?" Kate could hardly believe her ears. Her bedroom was *right there*.

"You're late for work." He continued to give her little pecks along her nape, up to her ear, along her cheek. "And you smell like airplane," he chuckled.

She swatted at his chest with the palm of her hand, *"What?"*

Adam just smiled, "You're late for work and you need to shower."

"That's it?!"

He pulled her toward him again, holding her close. "We've waited twenty years, Kate. We can wait another day," he said against her hair. Then he turned her around and gave her a little push. "Go get ready for work and I'll make you something to eat."

She stood still for a moment, in complete disbelief, watching him walk into her kitchen and take some things out of the refrigerator, as if this were any other day. As if she had not just come home after a humiliating cross-country overnight trip to see him. As if he had not just nearly ravished her against her living room wall. Well, he *hadn't* just nearly, had he? And that was the problem. He was rejecting her, *twice* in two days. "That's it?" she said. He looked up at her then, and his expression changed as he began to understand her agitation—well, her crossed arms and tapping foot would tell him something, wouldn't they?

Adam took her hands in his, but she continued to just stare at him, waiting for an explanation of some sort. She didn't realize she was still tapping her foot until Adam put his foot on top of hers. He leaned in and kissed her, just a peck on the lips that she didn't return. She felt petulant, but so what? "We've waited this long … "

"You said that already."

He kissed her again. "*I* have waited this long. I won't make love to you where someone else already has."

She said nothing, just looked him in the eyes, but she knew it was the truth, and she supposed she couldn't blame him for feeling as he did. At least for once his expression wasn't inscrutable. Satisfied, she turned away from him and headed toward the shower. "Try not to think about me naked in there," she said over her shoulder.

There were some types of hunger that a perfectly prepared egg white omelet couldn't satisfy. Kate had been so late getting in to work already, and yet the day still felt like the longest one ever. She couldn't stop texting Adam and still couldn't believe he was waiting for her at her apartment, as if he'd never left.

How did you beat me back to NY? She texted him.

Hitched a ride on a friend's plane into Teterboro.

So he hadn't had any of the hassles of connecting commercial flights like she had, she thought wryly.

She thought about their kiss earlier, how it was a far cry from and far more pleasant than the one in front of Claudia. She frowned at the thought of the other woman, the one who looked perfect with Adam.

She typed out a message:

What were you doing with Claudia?

She didn't press Send. She deleted it, then typed it again. Did it make her sound overly possessive? Part of her thought it was easier to ask him over a text; she didn't have to worry about what her expression might betray, didn't have to think that her voice might shake or sound accusatory. He didn't belong to Kate. In fact, he belonged to Claudia more than anyone. When was the last time she'd asked a man about another woman he was with? When was the last time she'd cared? *That would be never.* Just as she didn't think the game was over until the ring was on the man's finger, she also thought it was each person's responsibility to determine how attached they were—and to act accordingly.

She deleted the line again, then settled on:

How's Claudia?

She deleted that, too, realizing how stupid it sounded, as if to imply that she even *knew* the woman.

Kate took a sip of water, as if to erase the dryness in her mouth, which was the result of realizing what it was that she really wanted to know. *Why were you with her? Are you getting back together? Are you still in love with her?* Their kiss this morning had left little doubt that Adam was attracted to her. But Kate couldn't bear the thought that she might be his second choice, that despite their happy little home scene that she had witnessed, that Claudia might have broken up with him still. That some part of him was still in love with her and he was settling for Kate. It wasn't some misplaced sense of pride that was bothering her. She just couldn't stand it if she was his rebound. Kate wanted to smack her head against her desk. *Do you like her more than me?* This *thing* with Adam had practically turned her into a fourteen-year-old girl.

She typed again:

Are you and Claudia over?

She took a deep breath. This is Adam, she told herself. In a lot of ways, he knew her better than anyone else. She hit the Send button before she could rethink it and held her breath. Maybe it was a mistake, because at least if she asked him in person, he would be forced to answer. But then she couldn't bear it if he got that faraway look in his eye, that one that tells a woman that it's *not* over with an ex, not by a long shot. That same look that her father still got whenever Linda came up in conversation. That look of pain when Suzanne found out her ex was getting remarried. Kate had always told herself that she would never be on the wrong end of that gaze.

Kate stared at her phone, tapping her nail on her desk. If her hair hadn't been pulled back, she was sure she would have been twirling a strand of it. The thought of Adam touching her hair just hours earlier made her shiver.

Over.

A single word reply. Her heart began to swell and she smiled, in spite of her constant vigilance to keep her emotions in check—particularly at the office. And then another text came in from Adam:

Completely. I promise to tell you everything.

Kate was positively grinning at her phone now and was flustered and embarrassed when Jim came by her open door and said, "Aren't you coming?"

She looked at the clock—*shit!* Her distraction over Claudia/No Claudia made her ten minutes late to a staff meeting.

"Sorry—got caught up," she said hastily, not meeting Jim's eye as she grabbed a notepad and pen. She didn't even need them, but just needed something to steady her hands.

After the meeting, Kate was still berating herself for losing focus. But then she got back to her office to another text from Adam and she was nearly undone again.

Miss you.

She smiled and wrote back:

Should have thought of that before you kicked me out this morning.

Maybe you'll wear one of your sexy outfits later. (I do your laundry, remember.)

All my outfits are sexy.

Kate closed the door to her office and leaned against it. She opened a few buttons on her blouse and took a photo, showing just the right amount of black lace. She buttoned back up and opened her door, making sure anyone who saw her right then would see a stern, serious expression on her face as she typed a message on her phone.

Including the one I'm wearing.

You're killing me.

Satisfied, Kate turned back to her computer. She ought to get *some* work done today.

By the end of the day, Kate couldn't wait to get back home to Adam. But then a text came in from him, just as she was about to shut down her computer and call it a night.

Something came up. Will stop by tonight.

Kate was disappointed as she headed to her favorite deli to pick up a salad for dinner on the way home. Dinner for one. Of course she knew how to be on her own, but she'd gotten used to making plans with Adam and had especially looked forward to this evening, when they were finally going to have some time to themselves after this morning. Again Kate felt that tingle up her spine when she thought about it, his lips against hers.

She was still thinking about that kiss when she entered her apartment to find a note from Adam on her dining table. A note and an origami paper crane. Kate smiled at the memory that she didn't realize she still had. When they were sophomores in high school, there had been a Japanese exchange student at their school who had been on the math team with them. She had told them about a legend that promised that anyone who folded a thousand cranes would be granted a wish. And so during study halls, lunch hours, any free time she had, she could be seen folding paper cranes with beautifully colored origami paper. When Kate had finally asked her what she wished for, the student told her, on the condition that Kate would keep it a secret—she wished that she would find "love" while she was in the States, with a real American boyfriend. And of course, Kate had told Adam. They had kept the other girl's secret, but for the next few years they would tease each other about finding a "crane love" whenever one of them was harboring a crush on another classmate.

Holding the paper crane in one hand, Kate read Adam's note, enjoying the familiarity of his crisp, tiny handwriting.

> *I'm not sure how late I will be. But I promise to make it up*
> *to you this weekend. We'll leave tomorrow after the run.*
> *I've already packed for you.*
> *—A*

It wasn't that long ago that the thought of going away for a weekend with a man would put the feel of dread into Kate. She had always thought it was a slippery slope—a few dates, a weekend away, vacationing together. Soon one could be led to have expectations of the other. Expectations that were bound to be dashed sooner or later. This was different, Kate told herself. This was Adam, first and foremost, her friend. All the same, she read the note over and over again. Going away for a weekend might not be that big of a deal to him since he was probably used to going on all sorts of trips and vacations with Claudia. But to Kate this was a very big deal, and she suddenly felt like this thing might be moving too fast for her. It was one thing to seal the deal physically, but being together for an entire weekend—*away*? Sure, they spent tons of time together as it was, but she always had the option to get away, to do something else, to see her friends, to avoid more emotional investment than she felt comfortable with. Where was he even planning to take them?

Kate began pacing, still trying to figure out how she felt about his note, trying to tamp down the rising feeling of anxiety. She finally decided to get herself something to drink. She opened the refrigerator and found another note taped to a bottle of water.

> *Relax. It's just a date. —A*

Chapter 20

Adam looked forward to this morning's run more than usual. By the time he had taken care of everything last night, Kate had already gone to bed. Much as he had wanted to crawl into bed with her, he knew that wouldn't be the best way to start off this relationship. They needed to take some things slow, for Kate to get used to the idea of being with him, and not just physically. She needed time to figure out how she felt.

He still couldn't believe that she tracked him down in Palo Alto, that she had shown up on Claudia's doorstep just *yesterday*, after their stupid, stupid argument. He still felt bad about that, but couldn't keep from grinning when he saw her this morning, knowing that everything they had fought about was out of misplaced emotion. The fact that she felt something for him now, even if she wasn't sure what it was she was feeling, assured Adam that they could get past any harsh words that were said out of misplaced passion.

The glare Kate greeted him with was harsher than usual, and it was hard to suppress his grin. He could tell she wanted to say something to him, but was holding herself back. She was clearly used to calling all the shots in a relationship and clearly used to not caring if the relationship didn't go anywhere. Or rather, she was used to not wanting a relationship. "You were asleep when I got back," he said, understanding that he still needed to treat whatever was going on with them carefully. "I didn't want to wake you."

"*Now* you decide to give me space?" She plugged in her

earbuds and turned to the door.

Adam chuckled. He might have expected that. Good things were worth waiting for, he reminded himself. Kate apparently needed to learn that.

The routine of her morning run relaxed Kate. Especially today, she craved the comfort of the familiar rhythm of her feet hitting the pavement, the streets that she passed every day. She needed the stability of home because her feelings and certainly her actions the last couple of days had been anything *but* familiar. She thought she knew herself well, what she wanted, what she expected in her life. Finding Adam in her apartment yesterday filled her with a joy she couldn't (wouldn't) find the words for. And then he was gone again, and she had waited for him, flipping cable channels mindlessly, refreshing her Facebook newsfeed to see if he'd updated his status. She'd finally gone to bed when she realized she was listening to sounds in the hallway for the familiar click of his key in her door—it was just like when her father would light dinner candles as soon as he heard her mother's car pull in the driveway.

Adam could have told her not to wait for him, and then she wouldn't have. She would have gone out with the girls, or even by herself. She would have had a fine time out without him, just as she had before he'd come to visit. She would *not* have spent the evening waiting for him to kiss her again, wondering what he was going to tell her about Claudia, Googling "great date ideas" to find out what he was planning for them. She'd convinced herself that they were going to some local hotel, possibly with cheesy rose petals strewn across the bed. She mentally scolded herself—when was the last time she was asleep by 10 p.m. on a Friday night?

She was startled out of her reverie when she felt Adam beside her. She looked over at him, wondering if he was trying to say something to her, but he just looked straight ahead, apparently lost in his own thoughts. In another moment he had passed her, and she was startled once more at having to stare at his back, having him set the pace for the remainder of the run.

Where did he get those shoulders? She got a chill at the memory of feeling them under her hands, at the anticipation of feeling them again, only without a shirt between them this time. His sandy blond hair was cropped short in the back, and she ached to trail her fingers along his nape. She wanted him, without a doubt. She thought he wanted her too, but his behavior confounded her. It was usually so easy—find a spark, then act on it until the spark fizzles. Done. Why wasn't this easy?

By the time they got back to their lobby, they were both more out of breath than normal. "How did you get so fast?" Kate asked after a few moments, when she'd caught her breath.

"I have a lot of pent-up energy right now," Adam said, looking at her with an unmistakable hunger. He pulled her to him and kissed her. "Trust me, Kate. Space is the last thing I want between us," he murmured against her ear. He kissed her again, hard and fast, teasing her with his tongue, then pulled away before she could find firm footing. His kisses made her dizzy, made her world turn upside down. "Meet me down here in half an hour." She just stared at him, watching him go toward the elevator, *their* elevator that she should probably get on as well. But her feet were planted where they were, her legs were like jelly, and not just from the hard run. She didn't trust herself to move them. "And Kate," he called over his shoulder. "Wear pants. And no heels."

Forty-five minutes later, Kate was dressed. "To hell with him if he can't wait for me," she said to her reflection. The truth was, she'd spent way too long in front of the mirror, wondering if what she was wearing was right before discarding a top or pants for something else. It wasn't her fault she didn't know how to dress for some mysterious date. *An overnight date*, she reminded herself. She decided on a pair of dark skinny jeans, one of the only ones she had that were the right length to go with the ballet flats that had only been worn once. She chose a simple white V-neck T-shirt and threw on her favorite leather jacket over it.

Something told her she needed to be comfortable, and there was nothing softer than Balenciaga leather.

She walked into the lobby and didn't see Adam. Incredible. All of sudden he was keeping her waiting now? The doorman caught her eye and nodded his head toward outside. *Oh, well, I suppose it makes sense he might be waiting outside.* But when she stepped out, she didn't see him, at least not right away. Because why would she think that the guy on the *motorcycle* out front would be Adam? Harleys never did anything for Kate like they turned on some women. But this bike was different—sleek and modern, all clean angles in a bright cherry red. And when Adam lifted his helmet off his head and that mop of hair fell into his eyes like it always did, her pulse started to rev. She would never have pegged him as a Ducati man. A Prius maybe, something practical and efficient, though not exactly sexy. Was he just trying to impress her?

She wouldn't give him the satisfaction, though. She stayed rooted to her spot on the sidewalk until he held out a helmet for her. "New toy?" she said coolly, taking the helmet from him.

"Decided to bring it back with me this trip," he responded simply.

"How many surprises do you have in store for me?"

He smiled warmly then. "You'll see."

Kate slung the strap of her purse across her chest and got on behind him. "Well, let's go then."

Adam pulled her arms around him, and when she nodded OK, she tucked her body against his and they took off uptown. She could really get used to this, slipping her hands underneath his jacket, feeling the angles of his body. Minus the helmets and the clothes.

They zipped along the West Side Highway, but by the time they got to the Fifties, Kate was impatient. When they stopped for a light, she shouted, "Where are we going?!"

"I hear the leaves are nice this time of year," he called back to her.

She rolled her eyes. What was that supposed to mean? Was he taking her *out of Manhattan*? As if she hadn't traveled enough within the past few days. "The Plaza Hotel is right across town."

"Not my style," he said. The light turned green and any conversation was over.

Not my style, she muttered to herself. Waldorf Astoria, Essex House, the Mandarin Oriental, the Palace, the St. Regis, the Pierre. There were any number of five-star hotels just a stone's throw away, all with comfortable king size beds that gave them plenty of room to, you know, *maneuver*.

Kate couldn't tell how long it had been since they'd left the city, only that she'd been watching trees go by for a while now. She admitted they did look rather nice, the way their leaves were just starting to turn golden yellow. She could enjoy them a bit now that her heart wasn't lurching with every single curve on the parkway. She had had to remind herself that she was with Adam, the person she felt safest with, even on the back of a motorcycle careening further and further north from the security of her apartment.

Just as she started thinking about how sore she would be from this ride, Adam pulled off onto some smaller roads, winding his way through trees and more trees until they finally stopped. Kate had heard about all the state parks up this way, the Hudson River Valley wineries and lakes that made for romantic weekend getaways for the city people. She frowned a little as she took off her helmet and Adam took off his. "We aren't going hiking are we? I'm not that kind of girl."

"We just need to stretch our legs a little," he said. "Enjoy the drive?"

"I did," Kate answered honestly. At first, she most enjoyed just being near him, but then she really did like the scenery that didn't include tall buildings. She stretched out her arms and took in a deep breath of the fresh air that didn't offer the slightest whiff of New York City. Adam looked at something on his phone—checking to see where they were, Kate guessed.

He took her hand and walked on confidently, as if this had been the neighborhood playground he'd grown up with.

She loved the warmth of his hand, the firmness of his grip around hers. She found herself giggling. *I'm holding hands with Adam!* "Where are we going?" she finally said.

He just shrugged and kept walking. "Not sure. I heard there was a nice trail this way." He squeezed her hand and turned to her warmly. "Don't worry, it's not a hike."

They didn't walk for too long before Adam stopped to sit on a big rock, pulling her down next to him. They were alone as far as she could tell, with no others coming or going on the same trail. He still hadn't said much, but Kate sensed how he felt because she felt it, too.

"If anyone had asked me a few weeks ago if I could picture myself staring out onto a lake with you, I would have thought they were crazy." Yet something about it felt so right that Kate was almost afraid that speaking too much about it, about *anything* might break the spell. She tilted her head up to the warmth of the sun and closed her eyes. "How did you know this would be such a perfect spot?"

"I didn't," he said. "I read something about this area and thought we'd wing it."

"How very spontaneous of you," she murmured. She was really thinking how very un-Adam-like to not have planned every detail.

"There are lots of things you don't know about me."

"Good things, I'm finding." She kissed him lightly along his jawline. Had he always had that tiny freckle on his chin? She couldn't wait to discover everything about him.

"Mostly."

He'd kept telling himself that he was waiting for the right time, waiting for when she'd be ready. He'd planned this trip at the last minute, intentionally to get away from the city and all its distractions. He needed them to be able to start fresh in some ways, despite knowing each other better than anyone else did. "I need," he started, wondering how he'd be able to get any words out with her kissing him like that. "I need," he forced himself to say, "to tell you about Claudia."

Her body tensed a little, and he instinctively tightened his arms around her. He couldn't help but think she was on the verge of leaving him as it was, and now he was going to tell her all about his ex? Wasn't this conversation supposed to be taboo this early in a relationship? No, he told himself. He couldn't feel free to be with Kate, to let her know how serious he was about her, about them, until she'd gotten to know him. And his relationship with Claudia was a huge part of who he was over the last several years; she couldn't know him until she knew about his old life.

"When we first started dating, it was great. It was like everything just fell into place so easily. My friends loved her— hell, she was my best friend's sister. She's from the Bay Area and had lots of her own friends and family nearby, so I never felt guilty about the hours I worked, and she never gave me a hard time about it. We spent all our free time together, and before I knew it, three years had gone by. Getting married was the next logical step, so we got engaged. That was two years ago, but I kept saying I was too busy working to get married, and Claudia didn't seem to mind. But then her mom said something in passing. She'd said it as a joke, that I was quicker to decide what companies to invest in than I was to pick a wedding venue. But I knew she was getting nervous that Claudia was wasting her time on me." He took a deep breath. The words still didn't come easily to him. "So we set a date and they got to planning the wedding.

"I broke up with her two weeks before our wedding. It was supposed to have been this past May." He paused and looked at Kate. For once, she didn't have her emotions written all over her face. He was grateful that she was trying hard to just listen. "I just … moved out. I gave her no explanation, not a real one anyway. I left her to deal with telling everyone we'd already invited, her family, cancelling all the vendors we had lined up, returning the gifts, everything." He was choked by the guilt again. He'd gone over it all in his head so many times, but had avoided talking about it, saying it all out loud, until now.

"It happens, Ad. You can't keep beating yourself up about it. Cass tells me she sees it all the time—"

He cut her off. "She thought I just had cold feet, and I let her think that. I let her family think that." He swallowed and shook his head. "I'd known for months, maybe even longer than that."

"You didn't love her?"

"Not enough. At some point, I realized I loved her for her family most of all." Kate sighed, and Adam immediately relaxed. She'd seen his family—he knew she'd understand.

"Her brother was your friend," she sighed.

"Once we got engaged, I started calling her parents Mom and Dad."

"Oh, Adam." She stroked his knee. "No wonder you went along with it. No one would fault you—"

"I told myself that it was enough, that I loved her enough to marry her to keep the life we'd built together. And for a long time, I really believed it. But then I started feeling like there should be more, that it shouldn't have been so easy for me to spend so many hours working, away from her. I didn't want to rush home to be with her, I didn't jump at the chance to take time off, even when I could have. Hell, I didn't even come up with a decent proposal. I basically signed the receipt while she put the ring on. Who does that?!" Claudia had just assumed he wasn't good at showing his feelings, wasn't good with words. Maybe he wasn't, but the fact of the matter was, his feelings for Claudia hadn't made him want to try to be better. "She deserved—still deserves—better than that."

"Do you still have feelings for her?" Adam turned Kate to face him, knowing it wasn't easy for her to ask, so that she knew he was serious when he told her, "I'm not in love with her. I do wish we could have been friends, but that's impossible now." It was so easy for him to be honest with Kate, and when he saw her eyes fill with understanding and warmth at his words, he felt a surge of relief and excitement at the same time. "A few months ago, Claudia was convinced that I was going through some early midlife crisis, that if she waited it out, we'd be together and everything would be fine again. Hell, all of our friends were convinced, too, and no matter who I talked to, it was all the same advice—just move back into the house and work it out.

"I was so sick of it—I wanted more than 'fine,' and I was sick of hearing the same thing from everyone I knew. And I was too much of a coward to tell her that I just wasn't in love with her."

"I'm not sure which is worse—*I love you, but I'm not in love with you,* or *I love you as a friend.*"

"Exactly. But she wasn't getting the message until I finally told her about you."

"Wait, you told her about me *months* ago?"

"I told her about how I had this great friend from high school that I couldn't stop thinking about."

"Well, that would explain the warm welcome when I showed up on her doorstep looking for you."

Adam grimaced. "It was the second part of my realization—that I'd been thinking about you more than I'd been thinking about her. It was somehow easier to explain that I'd broken up with her for someone else, even though you and I hadn't even seen each other in years. I didn't know then that I'd be coming out here to see you, but I didn't want her to keep hoping that I'd move back in."

"So I was a prop?" Kate smiled. "To help you get what you wanted?"

Adam's mouth twisted upward in a smile he couldn't suppress. "I guess you could say that. Didn't quite close the deal, though. That's why I had to go back to Palo Alto this week. I'd finally decided to deal with all of our joint assets—a couple of bank accounts, the house. And yeah, for a while she was really mad at me and she was avoiding my calls. So when she finally called me the other night, I jumped on the chance to meet with her so that we could sign all the paperwork, so she would really know that it's over. That's what I was doing at the house—I was removing my name from the title so that it would be all hers."

"Oh God, and then I showed up?"

"It wasn't the best day for her."

"I'm an idiot," Kate frowned.

"I was going to tell you that I was going, but then you came home and picked a fight with me and I didn't get the chance." He kissed her temple. "I'm glad you came after me."

"I'm glad you came to New York." They kissed again, and Adam had never been happier. It felt right, being with Kate. This was what he'd been missing—*she* was what he'd been missing and he just hadn't known it for a long time. "Speaking of cold feet, though." He stiffened. He hadn't said any of that out loud, had he? This was all a lot to lay on her at once. He didn't want her to feel pressured at all.

"Yeah?" he croaked.

"My feet," she smiled at him, "are freezing."

He looked down. "Crap, that's my fault. I should've told you to wear socks." He shifted so that he could put her feet in his lap and removed her shoes to warm her feet with his hands. She seemed startled at the gesture. "Do you want to go?"

"No." She looked at his hands and then back at him. "This is nice."

He smiled. "Get used to it."

When it finally got too cold to sit around any longer, they decided to leave the park. "Now where to?" Kate asked.

Adam shrugged mischievously and got on the motorcycle. "I heard there's a nice place to stay around here. One of those old mansions converted to a hotel."

Kate ran her hands around him from behind and up his chest. "Now this is sounding like my kind of date," she laughed.

When they checked into the hotel, it was obvious that Adam had been in touch with the management, from the way the staff gushed over "Mr. Ward," telling him that everything he'd requested had been taken care of.

"Doesn't exactly sound so spontaneous to me, after all," Kate teased as they headed to their room.

"Well, I had to check it out first, didn't I? What if the place had bedbugs?"

Kate smiled, knowing he was only half joking. She gasped as they entered the room. It wasn't the vases of white roses everywhere, or the petals strewn across the bed, or the bottle of champagne resting on ice, or the delicious smell of food on the little table set for two. It was the sight of her Longchamp weekender sitting next to Adam's nondescript duffle bag that put the lump in her throat and threat of tears in her eyes. "How did you …?"

"I told you I would take care of it," he said softly. He put his arms around her waist from behind her, and Kate wondered how it was possible to feel content and excited and relaxed all at the same time.

"Careful," she said, leaning back into him with a sigh. "A girl could get used to this." He nuzzled her ear, gently kissing her, running his tongue along her neck. "Yes, a girl could *definitely* get used to this."

She turned to him, unable to put off pressing her lips against his any longer. She loved the taste of him, couldn't get enough of him. He took off her jacket, then his own, and his hands worked to untuck her shirt, unbutton her jeans. "W-wait," she gasped.

He pulled back. "What? What's wrong?"

"This is OK, right?" she chuckled, managing to muster a near-normal tone of voice. "Neither of us has slept here before, it's not my bed, it's not your air bed. This is it, right?" She couldn't help it. She *had* to tease him just a bit, make him wait like he made her wait.

Adam just groaned in mock exasperation, picked her up, and practically threw her on the bed, much to her satisfaction. She wasn't teasing anymore as he took his shirt off. She took her own off, eager to feel his bare skin on hers. *Where on earth did he get that body?* For a moment, Kate couldn't quite fathom that she was with Adam, her old high school buddy. But then it felt so right to be with him, the Adam she'd rediscovered, who knew her better than any man and adored her all the same. The Adam who was all grown up and, dare she say it, *sexy as all hell*.

They practically tore at one another at first, and Kate

couldn't get enough—not enough of the taste of him, the feel of him, just *of him*. Eventually they slowed down, and she took the time to savor the feel of his skin beneath her fingertips, the salty taste of his skin on her tongue. She relished the feel of his hands, confidently exploring every crevice of her body, with a touch so new and yet achingly familiar.

It wasn't until some hours later—how many, she had no idea—when they were in the shower together, that Kate realized what had happened, why she felt so *different*. She'd had great sex before. She'd had amazing sex before. What she had not had before was mind-blowing lovemaking. She wasn't particularly startled at the revelation. She'd known this thing with Adam was different, that what she felt for him was more than pure physical attraction. She'd never been more satiated, and still left wanting more. She was surprised at the intensity of her feelings, that she was more attracted to him because he was her friend, that she was more *in love* with him because, well, no one had made her climax four times in one day before. For the first time, Kate finally understood what Suzanne meant whenever she said she could never separate the emotions from the sex.

After their shower, Kate wrapped herself in a towel and glanced at Adam, who was beneath the covers of the bed. She felt a moment of self-consciousness when she noticed he was watching her, watching her face. This is ridiculous, she told herself. But she realized she didn't know how to act. Usually one person left when the deed was done. Or they just fell asleep. But she was too excited to sleep. Were they supposed to cuddle now? Was that what couples did? She sat on the edge of the bed, her back to him. My God, *I'm nervous.*

Adam propped himself up on one arm and reached for her. "Are you OK?"

"Yeah, I just want something to wear. Did you pack me any T-shirts?"

Adam got up and moved toward her bag, still completely naked. Kate blushed and averted her gaze. *What the hell is wrong with me?* He put her bag at her feet, then knelt in front of her. "Are you sure you're all right?"

"I'm fine, I am. I just … I think … we just need to get some clothes on."

Thankfully he turned away from her then and dug into his own bag. He put on some clean boxers and a pair of jeans and came back to sit on the bed next to her. Kate couldn't move and just sat there, staring at her bag, afraid to look at him, afraid of what he would see on her face, that he'd see how much she wanted him now, that her heart was practically bursting with what she felt for him.

He put his arms around her and held her against his chest, using his foot to stop hers from nervously kicking her bag. "It's just me," he said against her cheek.

She relaxed against him and closed her eyes with a sigh. "Oh my God," was all she could say.

Adam chuckled softly. "I know, Kate. I know."

She stayed there for a few minutes, nestled into his chest, until she felt like she could breathe normally again, when she didn't feel like she would go weak in the knees from just one look from him. It's just Adam, she repeated to herself. She kissed him on the cheek and then went to unpack her bag while he investigated the food that was now too cold to eat. "No one's ever packed for me before," she smiled.

"Hope I got it right," he said as he picked up the phone to call for room service. They were both ravenous now, and he ordered way too much for two people.

Kate grinned at the sight of her favorite pajamas, two matching sets of bras and panties, another comfy T-shirt from Uniqlo that was just like the one she had on earlier, her running gear, and another pair of jeans. He'd also carefully folded one of her more casual dresses and packed a matching pair of shoes. She found another pair of shoes tucked into the bottom of the bag beneath her toiletry kit. A pair of black five-inch platform heeled sandals with straps that laced up her calves. They went great with the black minidress she'd worn to a club opening. "And what exactly would I wear these with?" she asked, raising an eyebrow at him as she dangled them from her fingertips.

Adam paused from popping grapes into his mouth to look

over at her. He merely shrugged and said, "I thought you might miss your fancy things." He smiled. "They go with everything—what you've got on, for example. Or less." She went over to kiss him. His mouth tasted sweet from the grapes, and she wrapped her arms around his neck, lacing her fingers through his hair. She let her towel drop to the floor and sighed at the feel of his bare chest against her. She pushed him back onto the bed. "Room service is on its way," he groaned.

"No time for the shoes then," Kate responded, kissing his neck and chest.

They'd made the bed into a picnic spot, with plates of food spread out on all sides of them. Kate had thrown on Adam's T-shirt, the closest thing she could find when room service came knocking on the door. She sipped some champagne. "Your shirt's comfy. I could get used to these."

"No one makes them quite like Hanes," Adam said, his hand slipping beneath the shirt to caress her hip. She knew how he felt because she couldn't stop touching him either, finding pleasure in even the most innocent touches—when her knee touched his as they sat cross-legged on the bed, or when their fingers touched as they both reached for the same bread roll.

"I still can't believe we're here," she said, studying his eyes, every angle of his face in a whole new way. "How did you know?" she asked softly.

"That I was falling for you?"

"That I would fall for you."

"Isn't falling in love what everyone wants?" He leaned back against the pillows with one arm behind his head, pulling her down to lie next to him.

Love. He'd said it. She waited for that familiar feeling to come, that urge to flee as soon as a guy started getting too attached. The feeling never came, just an odd warmth in her chest, a sensation that felt safe and intoxicating all at once. "I thought love was for other people."

"You didn't always think that way." She looked at him quizzically. It had certainly been that way for as long as she could recall. "You used to read romance novels, remember? Those Harlequin things?" She laughed, she *did* remember now, especially about how her mother would tell her that smart girls didn't read those kinds of books. "You must believe in love. Somehow you just stopped believing it could happen to you, and I decided to prove you wrong." He gave her a self-satisfied smile.

She looked into his eyes, so filled with the happy disbelief that there was someone who knew her so well—and liked her anyway. "I can't believe you remember I read Harlequins. It's been years since I picked one up."

"You hid some in my backpack that time, remember? So Linda wouldn't see them. My father almost got the belt out when he found them, until I explained they were yours."

Adam's expression darkened at the mention of his father. She shuddered at the image of scrawny high school Adam getting hollered at by the giant of a man she remembered. "Sorry. I don't think you ever told me that part."

"My father was—still is—a Neanderthal."

"Must not have helped that your best friend was a girl." She didn't take her eyes off him, not wanting to miss anything his expression might tell her, even if she had to interpret what he *didn't* say to know how he felt.

He shut his eyes for a moment, as if closing them against the bad memories. He shook his head no.

"My parents always liked you," she said. Whether she was trying to make him feel better or to shift the topic from something clearly still so painful to him, she wasn't sure. "Dad thought you were such a gentleman, and Linda thought you were smart as a whip."

"Your parents saved me, you know. Sometimes the snacks your dad would make for us after school were the only reason I didn't feel hungry that day. And your mom wrote a recommendation for me when I was applying to colleges."

"I kind of knew about the food—it was hard not to see that you practically shoveled sandwiches into your mouth! I never knew about the recommendation, though."

"She didn't want my dad to find out since he would have twisted it into being a handout of some sort and gotten mad.

I didn't even ask her to do it; she just handed me an envelope one day with a letter inside." Kate felt a swell of pride about her mother. Linda may not have been the most maternal parent in the traditional sense, but she did her best with what she was good at.

"Will you go back to Ann Arbor for Thanksgiving?"

"I haven't spent the holidays there in years, but I guess it depends."

"On what?"

"On whatever you're doing."

He said it so nonchalantly, as if making holiday plans weeks in advance were a perfectly natural thing to do. Maybe it was for some couples, and Kate knew that they were indeed a couple now. But she couldn't recall the last time she'd made plans so far ahead of time with a man before and felt her body tense against his. "You should do whatever you usually do …"

Adam ran his fingers along her hairline and cupped her face in his hand. "You're mine now, Kate," he said matter-of-factly. "I'm not going anywhere, so you may as well get used to me."

Kate snuggled back into Adam's chest so that he couldn't see how much she was grinning now. She wondered when this giddiness would fade. Maybe when he went back to California, she realized. He couldn't stay in New York forever.

"I'm not going back, in case you're wondering," he said, once again startling her with his uncanny ability to read her thoughts. "Not permanently anyway, so you really can get used to me."

"Don't you have a business to run? Computers to build?"

"I haven't built a computer in years," Adam smiled. "Anyway, I've found that teaching agrees with me. And the school seems to like me enough, so I'm going to be teaching two courses next semester."

She wrapped her arm around him tighter; she couldn't be any happier. "You won't miss sunny California?"

"I'm still going to wear my flip-flops, no matter what you say."

Kate chuckled and put one of her legs over his. "I've decided I like your toes after all."

Chapter 21

On Monday, Kate was resolved to get her head out of the clouds and back into work. She was almost successful until she got a text from Adam:

Mom broke her leg. Going to Ann Arbor tonight.

It must be serious for Adam to go back. He tried to find any reason to stay away. She barely thought about it before typing back:

I'll go with you.

She looked at her work calendar. It would take some juggling, but there wasn't anything she couldn't reschedule.

Adam's text came in:

Are you sure? You'd need to leave by 5 to catch flight.

She responded without hesitation:

As long as you can pack for me.

Kate told her assistant that she'd be leaving early and would be gone for a couple of days for a family emergency. For the rest of the afternoon, Kate was a model of efficiency, returning calls, managing meetings through phone or web. It was an odd feeling for her, to have something come up outside of work. For a moment she felt guilty, but then she told herself that it was no different than the times colleagues had to attend to a suddenly sick child. All the same, she resolved to show more sympathy to Rachel.

The only crinkle in her plan was when the boss came

striding down the hall at around 4:30, telling the managers to gather in the conference room for a "brainstorming" to kick off the week. Kate was in the middle of another conference call that she was trying to jam in before 5:00, and there was no way she could pop in to the boss's meeting for just a few minutes and then excuse herself. There wasn't even enough time for her to be berated after telling the boss she couldn't stay. So she did something she'd never done before. She left. When her call was over, she instructed her assistant to go to the conference room to tell the boss she had another meeting and that she would be out of town until Wednesday for a family emergency. All of it was true, Kate reminded herself, and forced herself to ignore the rising lump in her chest as she raced toward the elevator.

When Kate got to her apartment, she saw their two bags packed and ready by the front door, and Adam had already scheduled a car to pick them up to take them to LaGuardia. She'd learned her lesson from the last time she hopped on a flight at the last minute and went to her bedroom to change into a pair of skinny black pants, a grey fitted T-shirt, and some wedge heeled pumps. She knew there was no need to check her bag to make sure all her necessities were packed, so she took the few minutes she had to brush out her hair. Updos didn't travel well, and Adam seemed to like her hair down better, anyway.

In the car, Adam filled her in on his mother's condition. She'd fallen on the steps after tripping over the grandkids' Matchbox cars last week. She was lucky she'd only had a minor fracture in her left leg, but apparently there had been some complications during the healing process. Adam hadn't even known about the incident until today, on the rare occasion when he decided to call her.

"I keep telling her she runs herself ragged taking care of my brothers' kids every day. Five boys are too much for her at her age, and they're spoiled rotten. I offered to hire someone to help her, but she just says, 'I raised five boys once, I can do it again.'" Adam shook his head in frustration. "I think she would take the help if not for my dad and his damn pride. This shouldn't have happened," Adam said angrily.

"So you're going there to check up on things?"

"Basically, yeah. I can't tell if things are worse than she's letting on or what. It doesn't sound like she can walk at all yet, and I can't imagine my father's too happy about that."

"How long has it been since you've been there?"

"Two-and-a-half years," he said sadly, with a deep sigh. Adam took her hand then and gave it a soft squeeze. "I'm glad you're coming with me."

"Me too," Kate said. She kissed him lightly on the lips, and any hesitation she felt about leaving work was gone.

It felt a bit surreal to be driving through Ypsilanti with Kate, on their way to his house, his *parents'* house. As they pulled up to the house, Adam had to take a few breaths before he could get out of the car. It hadn't been an *unhappy* childhood exactly, just a misunderstood one of his father's version of tough love. He squeezed Kate's hand again, feeling none of the nerves he felt when he'd brought Claudia here. It had been the first and only time she'd met his family, and it had been the last time he'd been here—all at Claudia's insistence. The house was a modest three-bedroom split-level, which was the perfect size for empty nesters, but growing up with four brothers, it never felt big enough.

Even so, Adam was amazed at how small it felt now, as he and Kate stood in the threshold of the front door while his mother kissed them hello and remarked about how gorgeous Kate was, even though she was all skin and bones. He tried to contain his anger at the fact that his mother answered the door, hobbling on a rolling walker, while his father was in the exact same position Adam remembered while growing up— slouched on the old leather couch with his feet up in front of the television. His dad did get up at least to greet them when he noticed Kate.

"Good to see you with a nice, local girl, son," he said gruffly, looking at Kate. His father turned to him with a look that passed as warmth for John Ward. "I don't remember you being so tall, kiddo," he said. "Still scrawny though, eh? Not like your pop here, with the old Ward belly," he laughed, patting his stomach that now hung over the waist of his faded corduroys. His dad pat him on the back. "It's good to see you." Then to his mother, he barked, "Mary, get the kids something to eat. They've come all this way." Adam cringed.

"No, no, please don't get up," Kate said to his mother. "We're fine actually, we grabbed something on the way." His mother protested and his father just frowned until finally they were placated when Kate and Adam brought over some cookies and glasses of water and brought them to the kitchen table to sit with his mother while his father resumed his position on the couch.

Adam wanted to get the full story from his mother, but she was clearly too distracted, apologizing for the mess, for not having the tea kettle on. "The girls come over to help sometimes, but you know how it is, it's not their house." Adam looked around and noticed that there was more than just the usual comfortable clutter of knickknacks that he had grown up with. There were empty cookie and cracker wrappers lying on every surface, the sink was full of dirty dishes that looked like they'd been there for days. The trash hadn't been taken out, and there was a small stack of pizza boxes next to it. The worst, in Adam's view, was the slew of toys all over the floor, including those damn metal cars belonging to his nephews.

Kate, thank goodness, had noticed as well, and was quietly throwing out trash into a plastic bag that had been lying around. "The kids are old enough to pick up after themselves," Adam said tersely.

"Oh, you know how boys are, so busy running around. They're just like you when you were young." She chuckled. "Well, maybe not *you*, but just like your brothers."

"Let me get you someone to help out with the house, to do the dishes, vacuum ..." His mother glanced at his father, who was still fixated on the television.

"Oh, you know your father doesn't like strangers in the house."

"Then get my brothers to help you. It's their kids you take care of—they can at least pitch in." Adam's voice was louder than he meant it to be. "For God's sake, Ma, you've gotta get off your feet—"

His father got up then and stood over him. "Listen here, hot shot, we all work around here. I work, your brothers work, their wives work, and we work hard. We all have our jobs to do and your ma takes care of the kids and the house, just like she did when she took care of you boys."

"Just let me get her some help, just for a while until her leg heals."

His mother looked away as his father turned red with anger. "You don't come into my house and think you're going to throw your money around. I've taken care of my family for a long time, in case you forget."

"I didn't mean it that way," Adam said, looking at the table. He was grateful Kate had moved on to the dishes and hopefully couldn't hear him being reduced to a teenaged boy again.

"Good," his father said and turned to go back to the television. "Now have a nice visit and don't upset your mother anymore." As if to prove a point, he said, "Mary, I need another can of pop, please."

Heat rose into Adam's face, and he covered his mother's hand with his to keep her at the table. "He can get it himself," he said through gritted teeth.

"Don't get his back up, Addy." *Don't get his back up, don't press his buttons, he's just tired, he works so hard.* The myriad of his mother's excuses came flooding back, and Adam felt his temper flare.

Then Kate was next to him, pushing a can of pop into his free hand. He looked up at her and she shook her head at him. She was right. His father was not going to change. He took a breath and took the can of soda from her. He set it none too gently on the coffee table in front of his father without a word.

"Maybe *you* should come and help your mother out."

Adam felt his face flush with guilt and was glad his back was turned against his father. It really had been too long since his last visit, and the only reason he came at all was for his mother.

He spent a few more minutes chatting with her, until she all but shooed them out the door, telling him his brothers would be there soon and it was more ruckus than she could handle already. She smiled when she said it, and he knew she loved "the ruckus" on a normal day. But she also knew there was no love lost between him and any of his brothers, so he didn't even ask which ones were coming or if he should stay to see them.

He and Kate said their good-byes and stepped outside. Already he could breathe easier, feeling the tension leave his shoulders—until a minivan pulled up to park in front of their rental.

"Runt! Hey, Runt, is that you, buddy?"

Through clenched teeth, Adam responded, "Hey, Mike," as his oldest brother got out of the driver side of the van. "Hi, Rose," he said to his sister-in-law as she struggled to carry a large pizza box, a six-pack of soda cans, and to open the back doors to let out their kids, all boys, aged four to eight. His brother caught him in a bear hug, giving him a noogie while he was at it, even though he had to reach up a little to do it now.

"Is that Katie?" his brother said, releasing him. "You grew up all right, didn't you?"

Kate just gave him a tight smile, and Adam excused the both of them, eager to just get back in the car and drive away.

A few minutes later, when they'd both had a chance to breathe easier, Kate said, "I'm sorry that didn't go that well."

Adam just shrugged. "I got what I needed. Michigan's playing Ohio State on Saturday. The house will be empty except for Mom. That's plenty of time to get some people in to clean the house and deliver some groceries."

"Your dad won't know? And your mom won't mind keeping it from him?"

"My dad doesn't know a lot of things. I paid off their mortgage, got the car fixed." Adam smiled. "I was on the math team, not the swim team."

"Really?! He never knew that?"

Adam shook his head. "Or he was in denial. My mother let me be who I wanted, she just didn't want me to make waves. It was brilliant, really. Dad was OK with any sport I was willing to take up, but swimming's not something he'd ever want to watch, so we didn't have to worry that he'd turn up at a meet or anything."

"Your mom is really something," Kate said softly.

"Yeah, I know."

Kate got dressed in their hotel room with a heavy heart the next morning, as she prepared for their visit with her dad. He'd been a great father growing up, packing her lunches with happy faces on the brown bag, driving her from one extracurricular activity to another, helping her with projects when she needed it. The kind of involved dad that few kids she knew had back then. But since the divorce, he'd become a shell of that man, and it had become tiresome to be his amateur life coach—tiresome until time and distance made their relationship more like distant relatives than father and daughter.

She wasn't even sure if he knew she was "engaged," whether or not it was something Linda would have mentioned to him. She decided she wouldn't bring it up today, a little afraid that he would sense that something was amiss, that he would probe with his keen writer's sense that there might be more to the story than she was willing to divulge to him.

From the way her dad grinned at her and Adam as they slid into the diner booth across from him, it was obvious that he was glad to see them *both* and obvious that mentioning an engagement with another man would have confused him. Kate took great pains not to touch Adam, not to twine her fingers with his or put her hand on his thigh as it seemed so natural to do. But from the way Henry Wallace kept looking from her face to Adam's and back again, she knew this man still knew her as well as he did when she was thirteen, when she came home from a party where they played spin the bottle and experienced her first kiss. Her dad would never embarrass her by asking if they were dating, he would wait her out until she was ready to tell him for herself. But Kate wasn't thirteen years old anymore, and she

Wendy Chen

wasn't ready yet to put this thing with Adam, whatever it was, into words for anyone.

She kept the conversation to small talk, and Dad thankfully followed her lead. "How's your mother?" he asked then. "Are you seeing her on this trip?"

Kate shook her head. Dad just nodded and said nothing. "It was an unexpected trip and she's just started the semester—" she trailed off, knowing the excuses sounded hollow, realizing her dad needed no explanation, that he had made those very same excuses to Kate for years. She missed him, she realized. But she didn't miss seeing the cloud of sadness that still lingered around him, a sadness that had nothing to do with his age.

Before long, it was time for her and Adam to leave for their flight. She was surprised when her dad pulled her in for a hug as he walked them out to their car. "Adam's always been good for you, Katie girl," he said into her ear. Before she could respond, he'd tugged on her ponytail and said "Have a good trip back" to the both of them. She didn't even mind that he'd mussed her hair in the process.

Chapter 22

Kate went straight to work from the airport, even though most of the day was gone. She'd brushed out her hair and put on makeup in the cab and again praised the benefits of black sheath dresses for hiding wrinkles. She walked quickly into her office and turned on the lights, as if she'd just returned from a particularly long meeting. But as she started up her computer and checked her voicemail, her assistant clung to her doorframe. "He wants to see you," she said. Kate took a deep breath. *This doesn't mean anything*. She nodded and absentmindedly listened to her voicemail as she gathered herself together.

The boss kept his office ten degrees colder than the rest, with intentionally uncomfortable chairs facing his desk. He kept Kate waiting, of course, while he stared at his computer for a few moments, *playing a crossword or Sudoku*, Kate mused. *Fruit ninja?* He was going to ask her about a client, just to see if she was still on top of things after her time away from the office. No problem, she'd been checking her email and voicemail while she was gone.

"Bed hair," he barked.

"*Excuse me?*"

"Thought you might wait until after the wedding before trying for a kid, but I suppose at your age—"

"What on earth are you talking about?"

"You think I haven't noticed, Kate, how well put together, how *professional* you are? Or had been. I notice that you've been putting in the effort, all buttoned-up, here, with clients. You've gotten serious about your clients, serious about your life. You have a successful career ahead of you." He sat back in his chair and waved a pencil in the air. "Or had one. I gave you some leeway, Kate. I looked the other way a few times when you headed out the door early, missed a few meetings. Your fiancé's connections might be very important to this firm. But what you're doing now—coming in with bed hair or not at all—I'd hate to see you go down that road all of a sudden."

Kate felt the heat rise to her cheeks. Anger, resentment, and admittedly a touch of embarrassment because a few days ago, she really wouldn't have been caught dead coming in to work with her hair down and mussed. She clenched her teeth and tried to keep her tone even. Professional. "I haven't missed a day of work in years. Not for holidays, not for sick days, not for anything." Her voice became steely, with barely concealed anger. "I cover for anyone else—*every*one else—who needs time off—"

"Whoa, whoa, whoa, Katie girl. Don't get so defensive." He gave her that smile, that I'm-on-your-side grin that the inexperienced fell for. "You're doing a great job. I just see the warning signs, that's all—"

"Warning signs? I had a family emergency. The only time I have ever had a family emergency."

He put his hands up, as if to surrender, his body language still all smiles and welcome. "We're a little family here, too, you know. I just want to see you succeed! You're almost a senior VP, you're so close. You've been so focused and now you're distracted. I'm just giving a little one-on-one advice—don't throw it away with this behavior." He gave her another smile and then looked past her. "My next meeting is here, Kate. We'll talk more later if you need to. I'm here for you, all right?"

Kate turned to leave, too much in shock over what had just happened, unable to look Rachel in the eye as she walked past, wondering how much the other woman had heard.

It was unbelievable. It was unprofessional. It was true.

• • • •

Kate had turned off her iPhone. It had killed her, hearing text messages coming in and knowing they were from Adam, so she had silenced it and stuck it in her bag. She still seethed at the unfairness of getting called onto the mat for her *behavior* over the past few days, when she had spent *years* building up a reputation for reliability and hard work. She stared at her computer monitor blankly, trying to keep her breathing even, swallowing the professional humiliation she felt. It angered her even more that this jerk had this kind of power, to put a halt to everything she'd been working for. She was so focused on her anger, she almost didn't see Rachel in her doorway.

Instead of the competitive, you-got-what-was-coming-to-you expression that Kate might have expected, all she saw in Rachel's face was compassion. "Are you OK?" she asked. Kate was nearly undone by the kindness.

"How do you put up with it?" She barely croaked the whisper.

Rachel looked behind her to see if anyone was passing by and then took a step closer into Kate's office. Just one step, as if it were risky to be observed talking about something other than work—which it probably was. Rachel smiled bitterly, "I spent five years out of the workforce when my kids were really little. I'm lucky I came back before the last big crisis, or I wouldn't have been able to find a job at all. My husband hasn't been able to find work, so he runs the house." She shrugged. "Our dickhead boss likes to remind me of that, but sometimes the evil you know is better than the one you don't." She paused then, as if realizing this was the first personal conversation the two of them had ever had. "Adam seems great. I'm sure you guys will figure this all out."

Kate remained silent. How had her life turned upside down in such a short time?

She watched Rachel leave her office. It was silly to think they would be friends; there was just no way in this god-awful dysfunctional environment they were in. She found a new respect for the woman, all the same. She sucked up the boss's torture in a different way than Kate did because she had different priorities. Rachel did what she had to in order to support her family. She wasn't out to compete with Kate, wasn't out to compete with anyone. Kate had never known what that felt like, to have people dependent on her, to shoulder that kind of responsibility, to put other's needs before her own. *To love someone that much.*

Kate's mind reeled for the rest of the day. Diving into her work was a welcome distraction from trying to figure out what to do about the rest of her life. She'd entered into a sham of an engagement as part of a childish whim that she thought would give her a boost in her career. And it had. Only it needed to remain fake. It was clearly impossible to have the career she wanted *and* to have personal life. She remained at her desk well past 8 p.m., long after all the others had left, after the boss had passed her office on his way out, giving her a nod of what could only have been approval when he saw she was still there. Even the cleaning staff seemed surprised she was there. And still she ignored the silence of her phone.

On the walk home, Kate rehearsed what she would say to Adam. The timing wasn't right, she couldn't afford to be distracted with a relationship right now, maybe after she got her next promotion they would revisit their status as a couple. And oh, by the way, could he keep up the sham engagement? It all sounded so awful, so selfish, even just in her own head. She turned the key in the lock of her door, still unsure of what she would say, the only certainty in her mind was that Adam would understand. He always did.

What she wasn't prepared for was a completely dark apartment, devoid of any smells of the spices from a recently cooked meal or any sign that someone had been here at all. She turned on the television to a news channel, just to break the silence. Confused and more than a little disheartened, Kate finally checked her phone. And saw them. Twenty-four missed texts and calls, all from Adam.

Have to go to SFO.
Next flight out is tonight.
Where are you?

Waited as long as I could.
Call you when I get in???
Where are you???

Her mind raced with the possibilities of why he'd be rushing off. Another personal emergency? Had Claudia called him back? Kate bit her lip. She didn't really believe he would rush to Claudia, though a part of her was afraid he was still more tied to their past than he wanted to admit. She was torturing herself.

The voicemail he left her was forty-five seconds long, and her heart pounded at the thought that something could truly be wrong, that someone close to him had been injured. She pressed the play button tentatively.

A friend's company that I've been backing … sued for IP theft … patent infringement … embezzlement … fraud.

The words came jumbling out in a rush, but it was the hurt in his voice that made Kate's heart sink. There was nothing worse than a scandal to kill a small company. Even some larger ones couldn't recover from something like that, even when the courts ruled in their favor. He was clearly taking this as a personal hit, and she thought again how much he understood her.

She sank onto the couch, staring blankly at the television. She didn't fool herself into thinking there was any advice she could have provided him, but she wanted to have been there for him after he heard that kind of news. What was he planning to do? How worried was he? It went without saying that he'd have the best legal representation possible, but if his friend was guilty, if he'd betrayed Adam's trust like that …

Why couldn't Kate have answered the phone when Adam needed her? Because she was too busy, too selfish with her own concerns. Kate snapped out of her thoughts long enough to process the next story segment being shown on TV. A Silicon Valley company investigation—and not just any company, but one that had previously been cited as an emerging leader in its segment, with an IPO speculated for early next year. Kate listened to the reporter's coverage, and there was no mistaking that this was the one Adam referred to as "his friend's company." It was worse than Adam had described. On top of a myriad other charges, the CEO had been accused of corporate espionage, for stealing hardware designs while working at a competitor prior to starting a new company, as well as paying off some of the competitor's employees to provide information about future strategy plans. He claimed that his investors—Adam included—knew of his actions, had encouraged them. Kate was thankful that Adam's name stayed out of the story, but she knew that would be little consolation to him.

Kate went to text him, even though she knew there would be no answer.

Watching the news. I'm sorry.

Chapter 23

Over the next two weeks, Kate barely heard from Adam, which was just as well, really, since she needed to get back on her game at work. She logged in more hours exercising, more hours at the office, and what little free time she had she spent with her girls. She and Adam would Skype sometimes, late in the evening before she went to bed. It was hard for her to see him, wanting him to share his burdens with her, but knowing his lawyers advised him not to talk about the case with anyone. They would chitchat about mundane everyday things. Whenever he tried to turn the conversation toward their relationship, she would change the subject. He stopped doing that after the first few days, as if realizing there were things better left unsaid, things they needed to talk about in person.

"Nothing like a face-to-face," her dad would say, whenever there was news to be delivered that they knew Linda wouldn't like. Whenever Kate needed extra money for glee club shows or other things Linda didn't particularly approve of, or when the stove broke and needed to be replaced, he would wait for her to come home, hand her a glass of wine, and work his charm in person to make it all right. Sometimes he would wait until bedtime, when Kate was already up in her room studying, and sometimes her father's magic would work and she would hear their laughter and low tones of cheerful conversation. Other times she would hear their voices raised, a door slam here or there. Either way, Linda would willingly write a check for her extracurricular activities the next morning.

Kate missed her dad, missed his quiet confidence. When her parents were still together, he was the calming influence over her mother, the one who assured Linda that they would get by, that they wouldn't lose their house, that Kate would have enough college money. It had been a long time since he was that man because much of his confidence left him when Linda did. It didn't help when Kate left for college either.

She decided to call him now, partly out of guilt, partly out of just missing him. She called him on his landline and sat in front of her computer as she walked him through signing on to Skype. It took a few tries, but finally his face was on her screen and he smiled with a grin so familiar to her, so genuinely happy to see her.

"I was thinking you'd be calling me soon," he said. "You actually took longer than I thought you would."

"Are you going to tell me what I'm calling for, too?" She was never good at keeping things from her father. Maybe she could pretend it was the old days when she'd sit at their kitchen counter and tell him about some boy who'd made fun of her. And he would immediately understand that it had been some *cute, popular* boy who she might have had a crush on if she'd been the type to have crushes.

"You remind me so much of your mother when you don't have all that makeup on." Her dad glanced away from the screen. Did he still have those old family pictures next to his computer? He used to joke that the collection of frames filled with Kate and Linda were his motivation to get back to writing, to sit his ass down and get some words out. But the way he looked away wistfully made Kate want to trash whatever picture of her mother was making him look so heartbroken. *Those road trips, those family holidays—those times are over,* she wanted to say to him. *Stop looking back. Move on.*

"How is your mother, anyway? Have you spoken to her lately?"

Kate swallowed and mentally pulled herself together. She wasn't a little girl whose daddy could make everything better. "She's fine. The same."

"Is she ... is she seeing anyone?" Her dad looked away again, as if he couldn't meet Kate's eyes. "I know, it seems odd, doesn't it, asking you about this kind of thing. It's just ... I'd heard, you know ... there's a visiting professor from London ... they went out to dinner."

"She didn't say anything to me about it, Dad."

"Oh, that's good. I mean, that's fine. She can do whatever she wants, I was just ... curious ... you know." He tried to smile then, but even over Skype Kate could tell it was forced. Is this what he thought about all the time? "So I was surprised to see Adam with you—"

Kate jolted back to the original reason why she'd decided to call her dad and knew that he was waiting for her to spill whatever she needed to say. "He came to visit recently."

Her dad's face stared back at her on her screen. She saw the sadness around his eyes more clearly than she did even in person. That was what love did to a person. That was what Linda had done to him. She couldn't do that to Adam.

"I thought we might ... there might be something there ... between us. I'm not so sure now, though."

"You always had a lot in common. And different in some good ways. You both have strong personalities. He's your equal, Kate, not someone who's going to let you run over him. You need that." And there he was. The dad who had cared enough to help her figure out who she was as a teenager and to let her leave home to find herself as an adult. But did he know how fickle she was, how selfish she was, how short-term and noncommittal she was? Of course he didn't; it wasn't a doting long-distance father's job to see all her adulthood shortcomings.

"I might not be what he needs." It came out as little more than whisper, but Kate knew her father heard her. His face hardened.

"When you find love, you keep it. Don't expect it to be easy all the time. You work at it. You don't give up on it."

And if he hadn't been glancing at her mother's picture the whole time, Kate might have believed him.

Chapter 24

Kate was good at suppressing how she was feeling, even to herself. There was one night, though, she'd just disconnected Skype and was sitting in her pajamas at her computer at 10 p.m. on a Saturday night. She didn't feel like going out, she didn't feel like doing anything. Adam had barely said anything, his mind clearly on the lawsuits, his hair sticking up from running his hands through it too much, the bags under his eyes clear evidence of the sleep he'd been losing. This wasn't happening to her, so why was she so down about it? She should be out at a party, or at least at a bar with a drink in one hand and a hot guy in the other. She almost snorted out loud at that last thought. There was no mistaking that she had no desire for anyone but Adam, even though every rational cell in her brain kept reminding her that she needed things to slow down with him, that she should be grateful for this break they were forced to have from each other.

Instead, she just felt sad.

She was reminded of something Adam used to say to her in high school whenever she'd get in the mood for a weepy movie or book. "Are you being hormonal?" From anyone else the question would have been downright rude, but he would ask it in such a guileless, genuine manner that it somehow made it okay.

Am I being hormonal? Kate pulled her pill pack from her bathroom drawer. She normally got her period by day two of her fourth week of pills. She was on day four. Still not late, exactly, but she felt her palms and forehead start to sweat. She found her phone and texted Suzanne.

Is it possible to get pregnant while I'm on the pill?

Her stomach dropped. Of course she knew the answer. Of course she knew there was always the smallest possibility.

You always use condoms, too, don't you? Came Suzanne's reply.

Of course. Except with Adam.

It just hadn't seemed … necessary.

What kind of pill?

Kate told her. And the next few moments waiting for Suzanne's answer seemed like an eternity. She stared at her pill pack. She was probably overreacting. Just because her period *always* came on day two of the fourth week for as many years as she could remember didn't mean she was pregnant.

When her phone rang and the caller ID showed it was Suzanne, Kate wanted to burst into tears right then. She didn't want to answer, didn't want to hear whatever it was that Suzanne felt important enough to call about. Why did she have to call a *doctor*, anyway? She should have called Cass or Mia, who would have told her to just calm down and wait for her period like a normal person. She could have just stuck her head in the sand like she did about so many other things.

Finally she answered, just before the call would go to voicemail. She didn't even say hello, just waited for Suzanne to talk.

"How late are you?"

Kate told her.

"It's probably nothing."

"But I *could* be pregnant."

"Anything is possible. Frankly, after thirty-five, it could be pregnancy as much as it could be early menopause." Kate almost made a crack about never imagining she'd be wishing for hot flashes. But she sensed there was more that Suzanne was trying to tell her. "The thing is, your pill was recalled."

"What do you mean *recalled*? Recalls are for cyanide-laced acetaminophen capsules or E.coli contaminated produce. What do you mean?"

Suzanne took a breath. "I looked it up, and it looks like a

bunch of your pills were recalled for—"

"For what?" Kate whispered.

"Inefficacy."

Kate couldn't remember how she ended the call, if she'd said a polite good-bye or thank you or anything. Only that she agreed to stop by Suzanne's office to get her blood drawn, the foolproof way to find out if she was pregnant this soon after missing her period. She somehow ended up in bed with the covers drawn over her head, taking deep breaths in and out. *What am I going to do? What am I going to do?*

One thing she could *not* do was tell Adam. It was an odd feeling because she had immediately wanted to tell him right away, just like she told him everything right away when they were in high school. But not this, not now, when he already had so much on his mind. She knew what he'd do—he'd come back to New York on the next flight, wanting to hold her hand while she got blood drawn. No, she had to at least wait until she was sure.

Kate had no idea how she got up the next morning, just that her body seemed to go through the motions of preparing for her usual run on its own. As her feet pounded the sidewalk in a steady rhythm, allowing her mind to wander wherever it would, she cursed that it was a Sunday, that she couldn't get the blood work done and over with. Even if Suzanne opened up her office specially for her, there would have been no lab open to get the results from.

She wouldn't go to work today, she decided. Sitting at a desk in front of a computer where she could Google "signs of pregnancy" all day would do her no good. She needed to keep on the move. She extended her run for thirty minutes longer than usual, until she was near exhaustion when she finally walked into her building. As fate would have it, she saw a pregnant woman in her lobby, wearing fashionable jeans and a cute tunic top that looked like something Kate herself would wear. Maybe the woman lived in her building, maybe she'd seen her a dozen times before—Kate had no idea. That day Kate noticed how happy the woman was, rubbing her belly while waiting for someone. It occurred to Kate that maybe she shouldn't have overdone it on the run, and she felt a flash of guilt for pushing herself. Would she have to avoid too much exercise from now on?

It was ridiculous, the way she was allowing her mind to wander when she didn't know for sure if she was pregnant. She couldn't talk to Adam, and she didn't want to talk to Cass or Mia either just yet. None of this was real, and talking about it would make it so. And yet if Kate had to spend an entire day with only her imagination to keep her company, she might go insane. So she took the train uptown to see the person who could keep her grounded for the next twenty-four hours.

"Pregnancy is not an illness. You can still exercise," Suzanne said flatly when Kate rushed through her door, saying she'd exercised too much and now felt faint.

"Do I *look* pregnant?"

Suzanne rolled her eyes. Kate sat on a stool at Suzanne's kitchen counter and put her head down on her arms. "I might have morning sickness. I feel nauseous."

Suzanne sighed and nudged Kate's elbow with a box of cookies. "You haven't eaten, you just ran who knows how many miles, and you're stressed."

"Your bedside manner sucks."

"You're not a patient."

"I could be!" Kate popped a cookie into her mouth. She was going to be huge if she had cravings like this. "I see babies everywhere now."

"It's the Upper East Side. You think there's lots of babies here, head across the park."

"What would I do with one?"

"You would make a great mother."

"*You* would make a great mother. *I* would just try not to screw up too badly."

"That's all anyone can do."

Kate swiped a chocolate crumb from her lip into her mouth. "What am I going to do?" she whispered. "I feel pregnant. I just know I am."

Suzanne just nodded, as if sensing that Kate just needed to speak out loud to let her own mind grasp the situation.

"I'm keeping it. I don't know if that surprises you."

"It doesn't." Suzanne smiled warmly.

"At least I know who the father is. I wouldn't have been able to say that a few months ago." Kate gave an uncomfortable fake laugh. Her love life was always the big joke among her friends, but this felt like anything but. "So I suppose that means I need to tell Adam."

Suzanne just looked at her. "Kate, you have to tell him. You can take some time until you're ready, but he has to know."

"He's really busy right now. I think he's going to have to move back to California—"

"Kate!"

Kate took a deep breath. "I was going to end things with Adam."

Suzanne was silent and then her expression softened. "It's scary, isn't it?"

"Being pregnant? Hell yes. Why do you think I'm here? I need all the medical counsel I can get."

Suzanne shook her head. "No, I mean, falling for someone." Now it was Kate's turn to be silenced. "It's scary, to not be able to control your emotions, to realize someone else's happiness and life can affect yours so much."

Kate felt the prickle of tears behind her eyes and blinked them back. She'd heard pregnant women got emotional. That must be what this was. "Why do so many people want to be in love?" Even as she said the words, Kate felt the hollowness in them. She remembered what it felt like to come home to Adam after a day at work, the way her heart swelled at the sight of her weekend bag packed perfectly with her favorite things, the contentment as she lay against his bare chest during their weekend away. And she thought about their trip to see his parents, how she wanted to brush the sadness from his eyes that was only there when he was in his childhood home, her feelings of helplessness now as he struggled to keep the businesses he worked so hard to build.

Suzanne looked at her with what could only be interpreted as sympathy. "It's so much easier to hide from your feelings."

"Your blood test results are consistent with those of an early pregnancy."

It had been several hours since the nurse from Suzanne's office called with that statement, confirming what Kate already knew in her heart. Suzanne had called when she had some time in between seeing her own patients, reminding Kate to make an appointment with her OB/GYN soon. She hadn't said as much, but Kate could tell from her tone that Suzanne was worried about her. With good reason, Kate thought guiltily. She had basically spent the afternoon at Suzanne's, alternating between immature selfishness and irrational terror. "How could this happen to me, what am I going to do?" she had wailed. And then, "What if I faint in my apartment and hit my head and no one ever finds me?!"

She had spent last night allowing herself to grieve for a bit, for the carefree life she wouldn't have any longer. She'd even basked in a few moments of melodrama, belting out songs from *Les Misérables*. Her situation wasn't quite that of Fantine, but well, she knew the words to her songs and found herself whispering them in the dark as she tried to lull herself to sleep. By the next morning, as the early light of dawn seeped through her windows and she realized she'd missed another morning run, the sadness had turned to determination. Determination that her life would change, but wouldn't be any less fulfilling. In fact, the confirmation of the blood test results was calming to Kate. She wasn't worried at all. In fact, her future and the choices she faced about her life, her career, seemed all the more clear-cut.

It wasn't cheap to raise a child in New York City, and Kate would need a bigger apartment for her and the baby. And a nanny, of course. Any thought she may have entertained about leaving her firm now was moot. No one would hire a pregnant woman. As it was, she would have to navigate her current environment carefully. She couldn't be fired; that would be a lawsuit waiting to happen, and even her boss was too smart for that. But she could be sidelined and her clients moved to others, as her colleagues anticipated her leave of absence. She needed that promotion more than ever, not just for her own pride and ambition, but for the little one that she was responsible for. It was a bit surreal, to be thinking about planning for someone that currently was the size of a poppy seed, according to one of those pregnancy websites that Kate found. Even if she wanted to live in denial, this tiny thing was certainly making its presence known. Kate pulled her wastebasket over to her side during another bout of nausea.

There was no doubt in Kate's mind that Adam would want to be a part of the baby's life in some way. But she would never use any excuse, not even pregnancy, as a way to keep a man or his money. She'd be able to carve out a great life for them on her own, and it would be up to Adam to decide how involved he wanted to be and for how long. Her feelings for him, whatever they were, were sidelined now. She had a single purpose, and that was to figure out how to give this baby the best life she could, keeping her own emotions in check while she did.

She still wasn't sure how she was going to tell him. Over the phone or Skype just didn't seem right, and she wanted to be able to experience his true reaction. She couldn't begin to guess what the range of his feelings would be. She had no idea how he felt about having kids. Maybe he'd planned on them with Claudia at some point, but was that part of the life they shared that he wanted to get out of? He seemed to like the kids at the barbecue, but that was just for a few hours.

What would Adam feel? She certainly didn't think Adam would resent her, at least not for long, and there would be no doubt in his mind that this was an accident. He could take some time to figure out how he wanted to deal with becoming a father. She wouldn't expect him to go with her to doctor's appointments, or make midnight runs to pick up food she was craving, or any of those other things normal couples did when they were expecting a baby. And once the baby came, he could see him or her as much or as little as he wanted. Kate caught another tear before it could drop. Grief for the kind of happy anticipation that other couples enjoyed was something else she hadn't expected. She took a deep breath and pulled herself together. There was a lot she could control about all this, she told herself. Worrying about what she couldn't control was a waste of time and energy that she couldn't afford.

Kate began typing to Adam. Sometimes it helped to gather her thoughts, to plan out what she would say. She described how she knew this baby was her sole responsibility, that she would love it with all her heart, that she promised to give him or her as great of a life as she could, that she would welcome Adam's involvement, but wouldn't rely on him. Kate was reminded of the notes she would sometimes write to Adam when they were in high school, when she couldn't talk to him on the phone for fear that he would hear her parents arguing over money in the background. She chuckled at the memory of his notes back to her. They were always short since there was always the chance his brothers would find him writing and ridicule him. But they were always carefully folded, with precise creases that carefully lined up the edges of the paper end to end.

By the time Kate had finished typing her thoughts, she had practically written an essay that included how thankful she was that he'd come back into her life, despite the resentment she may have expressed, and that there was no one else she'd rather be having a baby with. She reread it twice, three, four times over, tweaking a few words here or there, finding exactly what she wanted to say. If only she could read this to him and watch his face for her reaction, she thought.

And then Kate realized—the only reason she wanted to tell Adam in person was so that *she* could see how he would react. So that *she* would know how to treat the situation, so that *she* would know if he would be with her during the pregnancy (and afterward) or not. She hadn't wanted to tell Adam in person to give him the news in the way *he* would want. If she really had his interest in mind, she would deliver the news in the easiest way possible for him and then give him time to decide what he wanted to do. He wouldn't want Kate to see his initial reaction, she realized. If he were angry, or disappointed, or sad, he would want to keep those feelings to himself until he could figure out the most logical next steps for himself and get back to Kate with what those were.

She reread her letter one last time before copying it into an email message. READ WHEN YOU HAVE TIME she typed in the subject. She slowly typed in his name in the "To:" field and held her breath. She knew it was the right thing to do. He would read it when he had some peace and quiet, on his phone. She chuckled at the flash of worry that he'd read this news while he was driving—Adam was way too responsible to read and drive. He would be floored, that was for certain. But then he would have time to think, to deal with the news however way he wanted. Maybe he would seek out the friends he'd shared with Claudia, or maybe he'd deal with it alone. Most guys she knew would take this kind of news with a bottle of scotch. She wouldn't know when he read it, so he would feel no pressure to respond right away. She would wait for him until he was ready.

Chapter 25

It was time to tell Cass and Mia. Suzanne thought Kate might want to wait a while, a few days at least, to process the news with Adam. But no, the girls were her family and she wanted, needed their support from the very beginning.

Kate had asked them to meet her at an Irish pub in midtown, casual and centrally located so that no one had an excuse to not come. Not that they would have bailed on her. Kate had never been the one to call for an emergency girls' night before, having never had the kind of romantic drama—good or bad—that warranted the "I need you to meet tonight" text that she'd sent them after Adam's email.

The three of them were gathered at a small table, and the fact that there was a dirty martini in front of the empty seat assured her that Suzanne had kept her secret as she'd promised. At first Kate tried to make small talk as Suzanne stared into her drink, obviously trying not to let on that she knew the real reason why they were all here. How did one suddenly drop this kind of news? She really wished she could take a big swig of that martini. She didn't even know why she should be nervous because saying it all aloud might make it even more real?

"So what's going on?" Mia finally said. "Please tell us that Alberto's got his green card and you're calling off this engagement sham."

"Umm, no, not that." Kate was grateful for the interruption of a waitress coming by to check on them and took the opportunity to order a club soda.

"What are you, pregnant?" Mia tossed out.

Kate's jaw dropped and she felt herself flush. Cass and Mia gaped at her, and Suzanne just continued to stare at the table and bite her lip.

"Oh my God, I was kidding," Mia said. She grabbed Kate's hand. "I'm sorry, I didn't mean—"

"No, no, it's OK," Kate said through tears. "I'm OK with it, I really am. Not in my plans, obviously, but I'm really OK." She sniffled and someone, it must have been Cass, with her ever-ready bag of whatever anyone needed, handed her a pack of tissues. "I'm such an emotional wreck already, what the hell am I going to be like for the next nine months?" she joked. "It's Adam's, in case you're wondering." She saw them all glance at one another with some sort of knowing look and pursed her lips. The old Kate wasn't completely gone in a puddle of tears. "What, is it that obvious that I haven't gotten any other piece of ass?"

They all laughed then, and Kate forgot why she was so nervous about telling them.

"What did Adam say?" asked Cass.

Kate explained about the email, how she didn't know yet what his reaction would be. She thought they would express disbelief and disapproval that she would *email* news that was so important. But before they could say anything, she said they didn't know Adam like she did, that she had done the right thing for him by telling him this way. But that judgment didn't come, just those weepy looks and glances between them.

"This kid's lucky," Mia finally said, smiling.

"Why?"

"Because he or she will have parents who love each other," Cassandra finished for her as Mia nodded.

"I never said—" Kate couldn't finish as her friends just gave her knowing stares. "Even if I do, this changes everything. I can't just think about myself and pursuing my own happiness. I have to make sure my life is stable and secure for this baby, and I can't count on anyone else to provide that."

"Adam is a great guy," Suzanne chimed in.

"Who doesn't deserve to be tied down." Kate put her hand up when her friends were about to interrupt. She'd thought long and hard about all this, and she was going to maintain control of the situation. "He spent years on the path to marriage, in a relationship that was wrong for him. I'm not going to hold him back from whatever life he imagined for himself, just because he feels responsible for us. He still might find the perfect woman for him someday," she said shakily, "and I won't be the one who prevents that." She saw the girls give each other a look again, one that told her that they thought she was wrong. Kate couldn't take chances. Even if she wanted to see how things would turn out between her and Adam, there was too much at risk now. If they didn't end up together, if she didn't end up being what he wanted, it wouldn't be just her heart that got broken. Maybe this baby wouldn't have parents who were together all the time and wouldn't live with both of them like other babies did. But he or she wouldn't witness parents fighting daily or one storming off in the middle of the night. "We'll always be connected, especially with this baby," Kate continued. "As long as I play it safe, we'll always be friends." Her friends may not have agreed with her, but she knew they wouldn't argue with that logic, not now when what she needed was their unconditional support.

Their conversation moved on to practical matters then and promises to attend doctor's appointments and to babysit. This baby was going to have more than enough surrogate parents to care for it.

"Have you told Linda yet?" asked Cass.

Kate shook her head. "I'm going to wait as long as possible. You know I'm just going to be in for a lecture. If I can secure that promotion I'm up for, it might ease the news a bit. She might not think I'm a *total* failure." Kate chuckled bitterly.

"She might need some time to get used to the news, that's all."

"A couple of months ago, a friend of hers became a grandmother for the first time. She told me she didn't understand all the gushing about becoming an on-call babysitter. At the time I was relieved that she'd never try to pressure me to have a baby."

"If only our mothers could talk some sense into each other," Cass responded. "My mother's so eager for a grandchild and so happy that I'm finally dating someone, I don't think she'd care anymore if I got married first."

Kate was relieved to find a way out from being the focus of the conversation. Now that her news was out, she wanted everything to be as normal as possible. "So are you and Nick talking wedding bells already?"

Cass blushed. "It hasn't been that long. But there's definitely something different about him—about us."

"It's true then, that when it's right, you just know it?" Mia asked.

"Well you all know we had a rocky start," Cassandra chuckled. "It feels like he's The One, though" she continued softly.

Suzanne beamed. "I knew it!" she exclaimed. "Dum dum dee dum," she hummed happily.

They all laughed then, knowing Suzanne's eagerness to see her friends march down the aisle—as long as they were marching toward the right person. She was such a good person, Kate thought to herself. For as hard as Suzanne was looking for *her* One, and for as much bad luck as she had, she never showed any bitterness toward the others whenever they were lucky in love. Kate hoped that one day there would be a man worthy of her friend, who would give her the love and family she wanted.

"No way, no *way*, are we there yet," Cassandra interjected. "We haven't talked about anything of the sort."

"So if he asked you tomorrow, you'd say no?" Suzanne challenged.

"Well, I didn't say that—"

Suzanne smiled smugly.

"The biggest plans we've made are for the holidays. He's coming over to my family's place for Christmas, so who knows what he'll think of me after that!" she joked.

"I've been to your house for Christmas," Kate chimed in. "That is an *intense* time to be around the Hanley family!" she laughed.

"Well, you know my mother. Everything needs to be perfect for her, which ends up meaning nothing is, and all the skeletons in our closets come peeking out."

Kate could envision Cass in her shoes, sharing news of a pregnancy with a man who loved her and a family who would welcome a new member with eager open arms. She felt that stab of sadness again and shook it away. She could learn a thing or two from Suzanne—there was no point in missing something she had no control over.

Chapter 26

Kate took extra special care with applying her uniform the next morning, applying an extra layer of concealer under her eyes to disguise any evidence of another sleepless night. She added a few more brushes of mascara to appear alert and sharp and picked her newest suit, which was an obvious investment in her career. She had to negotiate and secure this promotion before announcing her pregnancy and had gotten a meeting with the boss at 8 a.m. She couldn't give him any sign that she had an agenda beyond her own ambition, lest he use it against her. It was hard for Kate herself to believe she had to play these games in this day and age when a CEO of a major tech company could announce her promotion and her pregnancy all in the same press conference. But the realities of mid-level managers were far different, as Rachel could well attest to.

As she sat outside his office, waiting the requisite five minutes he always made people wait, Kate sat up straighter and sucked in her midsection, wondering if she should have added a layer of Spanx for reassurance. She darted a glance at the boss's administrative assistant. It was always the women who noticed other women were pregnant first, wasn't it? She let out a slow breath and willed herself to rest her arms at her sides calmly, as she rehearsed her pitch and went through her mental bullet list of all the money she'd made the firm, all the clients she'd secured. She had to be careful not to ramble, to not allow herself to say anything extraneous, or even worse—emotional. As much of a ballbuster as she could be, she'd never had to advocate for herself like this before, having always been readily rewarded for her hard work in the past. This time was different, she reminded herself. It wasn't just her anymore; she had more on the line than just her own interests. She *had* to get this promotion.

His back was to her as she entered his office, as he typed rapidly on his computer. "So what did you want to talk to me about?" he said, not stopping.

Kate paused and her eyes narrowed. She had played this game before and refused to advocate for herself to his back. "I'll wait until you're done," she said lightly.

His eyes darted to her then and he gave a slight nod as he finished whatever he was typing a moment later. He swiveled to face her and clasped his hands under his chin. "I have another meeting in ten minutes, but until then, you have my full attention."

"This won't take long," Kate smiled confidently before launching into her pitch. She went through each bullet point in her head. How long she'd been at the firm, the amount of money she had pulled in, memorized by dollar amount. She didn't rush her words, allowing each phrase to sink in. "And that's why I deserve to be promoted to a senior VP position," she concluded. She folded her hands calmly in her lap and didn't break eye contact. She didn't smile, keeping her expression neutral and inscrutable. She raised one eyebrow ever so slightly as she awaited a response.

Her boss narrowed his eyes slightly and pursed his lips.

Kate refused to look away. She had mastered the pregnant pause, she mused.

A beat later he cleared his throat and sat back in his chair. "You've caught me off guard here, you know." This had to be another one of his mind games. It was no secret among anyone at the firm that Kate was gunning for a promotion. Kate said nothing. Would it help or hurt that she was eager for a new title? Maybe if he thought she was looking to jump firms, he might promote her to keep her. "Usually people—women—in your shoes aren't thinking about work that much."

"Excuse me?" It was Kate's turn to be surprised, stunning

her out of her silence. *How could he possibly know her condition?*

"Normally a bride-to-be is on the phone during the day, booking bands or caterers or this or that. Ducking out to see photographers or the like. Not you, though, Kate. I have to admit you've maintained your focus more than I thought you would under the circumstances." The boss sucked on his teeth. "Still, though, a promotion, new responsibilities ... that's a lot to take on while planning a wedding, isn't it?"

"I have never allowed my personal life to interfere with my work." Kate willed herself to remain calm. Was there even such a thing as getting wedding tracked? "Since you point out my upcoming nuptials, I want to point out that I signed two clients just in the time since I got engaged."

"Your fiancé certainly can be an asset—" He gazed up at the ceiling and then back to her.

Did he think Adam helped land her new clients? It was all she could to do avoid an outburst, tempted as she was to tell him off and walk out of here for good. But then what? She was stuck here. So she just let him talk.

"I'll think about it some more, Kate. You're a valued employee at this firm. Give me a few days to see what I can do for you."

"Great," Kate said with mock cheerfulness, as if she had all the time in the world to wait for his decision.

She spent the rest of the day ultrafocused on her work, eating her lunch at her desk, only checking for anything from Adam, ignoring her friends' texts and emails. Until her boss gave his decision, she wouldn't give him any reason, any excuse to doubt her work ethic. Just as she suspected he would, he walked by her office at 7:05 p.m., on his way out for the evening. As nauseated as she already was, the curt nod and wink he gave her on his way out made her even more so.

Kate arrived in her lobby exhausted. "It gets better," the man at the bodega had said sympathetically to her when she'd paid for her plain crackers and ginger ale. This only heightened her self-consciousness and anxiety. How long could she keep this secret?

Maybe she would call one of the girls to keep her company, to watch TV, take her mind off the worry. She opened the door to her apartment, surprised to find the lights on and sounds coming from the kitchen. She almost felt as if she were in a dream, to see Adam crossing the room to greet her at her doorway. She couldn't move her feet as she took in the sight of him. His hair was adorably mussed, though he'd gotten it cut quite a bit shorter than it had been. He wore his usual white T-shirt and worn-in jeans, but what made her nearly cry with relief was his smile, warm and reassuring.

Before she could say anything, he was kissing her, softly and sweetly, but with every bit of the same longing as she wouldn't admit to feeling until now. She dropped her bags to touch his face as he kissed her, to feel the two-day stubble that she'd missed, to trace her fingers along the curve of his nape, down to the shoulders that she'd leaned on for years.

He held her close, even after they'd stopped kissing, and she let herself lean into him, to bear the weight she'd been carrying. She closed her eyes and sighed. If only they could stay just like this, could shut out the rest of the world for a time.

"Happy to see me?" Adam finally said softly against her forehead. Kate could only nod, too afraid her voice would crack with emotion. Adam scooped her legs up tenderly and sat her on his lap on the couch. He removed her shoes and smiled at her. "You're not going to be able to wear these things much longer."

"No," she whispered, still too stunned by his presence to find her voice.

"And I probably won't be able to carry you around like that either." He made a gesture of a giant belly, making them both laugh as she swatted him playfully.

She stared into his eyes, just wanting to enjoy him, but she knew they needed to talk. "So you're not mad?"

He leaned into her, taking her face in his hands gently. "Mad, Kate? In the last few weeks, I've had a lot of time to think about what I want in my life. I lost my company, a friend I considered one of my best along with it, and possibly a good portion of my professional reputation. But what I've wanted the most all these years is a family." He looked into her eyes with an intensity that she'd never seen in him before. "You've been my family for so long, Kate, what could make me happier than another person to love?"

She couldn't help it then, she let the tears fall. And not elegant, controlled tears, but outright streams and sobs of relief. And when she started to apologize, he only chuckled and handed her a tissue. He kissed her again and said softly, seriously, "I'm sorry, Kate, that you thought you'd be alone." His words made her sob even harder with all the pent-up stress and emotion she hadn't realized she'd been feeling.

They sat together in silence a few moments longer as Kate nestled in his arms, letting herself bask in his warmth. For the first time all day, she wasn't nauseous, and her mind wasn't racing at all the potential disasters that awaited her career and her baby. *Their* baby.

"Come on," Adam said finally, moving her legs off of him gently. "We need to get you something to eat."

"It smells really good, whatever it is," Kate responded, suddenly hungry.

"Poached organic chicken breast and brown rice. I almost bought salmon and then thought you might not be eating that anymore."

"What's wrong with salmon?"

"Something about pollutants and being one of the types of fish pregnant women should avoid. Like swordfish, large tuna—"

"Am I supposed to know all these things?"

"When are you going to your doctor?"

Kate felt sheepish. When was she going to make time for a doctor's appointment? "Soon. He's impossible to get an appointment with." She sank down in a chair at her dining table.

"I'm sure they'll find a spot for a pregnant woman."

"I'll have to go during lunch or something. I need all the face time at work that I can get right now." She tried to ignore Adam's clear scowl of disapproval. "I still need that job, you know. I asked him outright about my promotion today."

Adam raised an eyebrow in what seemed like approval.

"Good for you. Did he act surprised?"

"How did you know?"

Adam shrugged and nonchalantly continued to plate their food and serve her a glass of ginger ale. "Part of the mind games he's playing. He pretends he needs time to mull it over, just to show he's got the power over you." He sat down at the table across from her and took her hand. "You'll get it, you know. And I'm glad you confronted him about it instead of playing his games."

Kate smiled. It felt good to have someone have her back. "I had to. No way in hell he'll promote me once I start showing. And do you have any idea how much it costs to have a nanny in New York?"

Adam's smile faltered then, and he pulled back from her a little. Kate realized she had relaxed too much with him. It was too soon to talk about what they would do once the baby arrived. "So how were you able to get back here? I figured you would be in California for a while longer, dealing with … everything."

A shadow crossed Adam's face again, so quickly that Kate would have missed it if she hadn't been scrutinizing his every expression. He looked her in the eye. "I decided to step down as chairman of the board." He must have seen the look of shock in her face because he rushed to continue. "It's fine. I decided days before you told me about … before I got your email. It's best for the company, to have new leadership, to create some distance from this scandal."

"You worked so hard to get to where you are. To have to leave it all for someone else to run—"

"It's just a company. I'll miss the people—some of them, anyway," he chuckled darkly. "But I have other businesses to keep me busy. After you told me about the baby, it sealed the timing of the decision. I'm making the announcement public tomorrow, about how it's a good time to focus on my personal life and impending marriage." His smile almost reached his eyes then. "Turns out this engagement comes in handy for both of us."

"Though, when it gets called off, it's all a bit more

public for you. You can spin it however you like, makes little difference to me."

Adam gave her an odd look then, which she couldn't decipher. *Oh, he didn't think he really had to marry her now, did he?* Before she could say more, Adam had gotten up to get her a second helping. Apparently she was hungrier than she thought.

They made small talk after that, until Kate could no longer stifle her yawns. "Why don't you go to bed?"

"It's only 9:30," Kate protested, even as she sighed at the thought of changing into her comfiest pj's and crawling under her blanket.

"If you're tired, go to sleep," Adam commanded gently. "I'll clean up."

She had to start listening to her body sooner or later, she supposed. And maybe if she went to bed now, there would be some hope of getting up in the morning for a run—a short, healthy run.

As he cleared up the kitchen, Adam whistled some pop song from when they were in high school, and Kate found herself humming along while she changed her clothes and took off her makeup. After she got ready for bed, she stood in the doorway of her bedroom for a moment, just watching him move around with such ease in her apartment. She exhaled another sigh of relief that he was going to welcome this baby as she planned to, that he was still her rock after all this time.

She must have fallen into a deep sleep rather quickly once her head hit her pillow. She woke up to her alarm at 5 a.m., refreshed and only slightly nauseated, to find Adam next to her. She hadn't even known that he was in her bed the entire night, she'd been in such a deep sleep. It was an odd feeling, to wake up next to someone and not want him to leave right away. Adam groaned at the sound of her alarm, and she quickly turned it off. He was probably still on West Coast time. "Go back to sleep," she whispered in his ear as she got up. "You don't have to impress me anymore." She laughed as he put the covers over his head in response.

Kate jogged three miles and almost, *almost* felt like herself.

When she got back home, Adam was still in bed, his head still buried under the blanket and a pillow, blocking out any sun that dared enter the room. She tried to be quiet as she got ready for work, when she heard a mumble from the mound that was Adam.

"What?" she said. "I have no idea what you're trying to say."

He shook off the covers then, and Kate couldn't suppress her smile at his adorable bedhead. And the fact that he was shirtless nearly took her breath away, tempting her to crawl back into bed with him. "I said, you need to eat breakfast," he muttered. "I put a granola bar in your bag." He lay back down in her bed then, and Kate chuckled at the dismissal.

She was the first to get in to work, just as she had planned, and had turned on all the lights in the main areas. It was too depressing to be surrounded by darkness while she scrolled through pointless email messages that her boss had sent late last night. He'd been testing her, she was sure, to see how quickly she would respond to ones sent at 9:57 p.m., 10:35 p.m., then at 11:02 p.m. She mentally kicked herself. She should have known he would do this. His messages requested her thoughts on a recent report put out in a trade publication, asked the status of a client who had been thinking about signing on with the firm, asked her opinion about the performance of a junior employee. There was nothing that could not have waited until business hours, but still she could envision him preaching about the importance of responsiveness.

Linda had always told her that it was twice as hard for women to prove themselves in business, that men would be praised for taking time off for family needs while women would always be reprimanded for the same. Kate crafted a response to the boss, answering his questions in one thoughtful message, to make it easy for him to remember what he'd asked her in the first place. She closed with an offer to follow up in person should he wish to meet at any time and hoped that the thoroughness of her answer would make up for the lack of one-liner responses he probably anticipated during the night.

She wondered if Linda had ever had a boss like hers at some

point in her career. Her mother often came home in less than happy moods, but she remembered one time in particular, when a colleague had received tenure over her mother, how Linda had vented to her father about how ridiculous it was to think that women could not be the primary breadwinner in 1988. She remembered how her father had tried to make Linda laugh off her anger, how he'd told her about all the writing he'd been able to get done that day, including a satire about academic life. Linda had lowered her voice then, unaware that Kate could still hear her from another room. "Kate has such potential," she had told her father. "She won't be held back like I've been."

Kate felt a rush of empathy for her mother, as she wondered what Linda would do in her position. Knowing that a promotion was imminent yet illogically precarious, she would have been checking her work messages well into the night. Kate swallowed guiltily.

She decided to call Linda's office then, knowing her mother would more likely be at the university than at home, knowing that the call wouldn't last for more than five minutes, as both women needed to get on with their workdays. Kate was actually surprised at how pleased her mother was to hear from her.

"I was just thinking of you, actually," Linda said, against the sound of shuffling papers in the background. Kate could just imagine her trying to organize her desk while she held the phone receiver against her shoulder. "I wondered if you'd thought about the prenup yet."

"I don't think I'll need one, actually." Kate paused and found herself surprisingly at ease with what she was about to say. "It's Adam, mother. I'm marrying Adam."

Linda laughed. "Well, why didn't you say so from the beginning? I'm surprised he isn't pushing *you* for a prenup."

"You know he's … successful?"

"I've been keeping tabs on that boy since the two of you were in high school. A shame about the scandal right now, but I'm sure it will blow over soon enough." Linda paused, and Kate felt her full attention shift to the conversation. "I'm sure he's turned out to be a wonderful man, Kate. You two always got along so well."

Kate felt tears threaten. It would be hard to tell Linda if they decided not to get married. *When* they decided not get married. "Yes," was all she could manage to choke out.

"The thing with successful men, though, is that there are always other women waiting in the wings for them."

"Don't worry, Linda, I'm still going to have my own career. I'm not going to give up my life to be with him."

"It'll be hard, you know. It'll start off as little things; you won't even see it coming—"

"I'm up for a promotion," Kate blurted. She hadn't intended to tip her hand, but she couldn't, just couldn't, endure a lecture about a marriage that wasn't even going to happen. As she anticipated, her mother was thrilled.

"It'll be great to get that in the bag before you get married. I'm proud of you," Linda said seriously. "You were always smart, but you grew up and got practical."

Not like your father, Kate added silently.

"Sheryl Sandberg is right about all this *Lean In* business, you know. I didn't want to say anything before. But now that you're up for a promotion, you have real leadership potential."

If I can avoid getting mommy-tracked. "Thanks," Kate gulped. It felt odd to receive such high compliments from Linda, and Kate hoped she'd be able to avoid disappointing her mother. Single motherhood certainly wasn't what Linda envisioned for her.

Kate ended the call before she could blurt out more life details that would have to be revised later on.

Who's your doctor? read the text from Adam.

Kate replied with the name and phone number. If he was going to insist on helping her, she may as well let him. And it was nice to have someone in this with her. The girls had been great, but no one really had the time to read *What to Expect When You're Expecting* just out of moral support. Heck, Kate hadn't even read it, though she did download it to her Kindle at least.

About ten minutes later, Adam texted again.

Appointment TODAY at 12:30. DO NOT MISS IT. I will meet you there.

Kate chuckled at first at the directive. She hadn't made any plans at lunch outside of working at her desk, but it wouldn't be the first time she missed an appointment. And then her throat began to dry, not from nerves about seeing a doctor, but about Adam coming with her. He was really in this with her. What, was he going to just approve a press release that would change his entire career and then hop on over to sit with her in a waiting room?

That is exactly what Adam did.

"You don't have to be here, you know," Kate said over her shoulder to Adam next to her.

"Well, I thought one parent should want to be here," he responded sarcastically.

She looked up from her phone then. "I just meant that I could do this on my own. I mean, I don't think much happens at this first appointment. It's not like the baby is going to wave at you or anything."

"Well, no, it—I mean, he or she—doesn't have hands yet. But her heart will beat for me." He said it with such an adorable smile, how could any girl's heart not beat for him? Kate swallowed and changed the subject.

"I don't know how you can stand it, not looking at your phone for news, to see what people are saying about you," Kate said to him as he flipped through a month-old magazine in her doctor's waiting room.

"This is important."

"You could still multitask."

Adam nodded toward Kate's smartphone that she held in her lap. "So I can curse Autocorrect as I compulsively respond to messages, all of which can wait an hour?"

"If I reply now, then I won't forget to do it later."

He chuckled at her and reached for another magazine. "Are you going to take conference calls in between contractions?

Because people will probably hear your breathing a little too much."

Kate swatted him on the arm and couldn't help but laugh herself. "The Marissa Mayers of the world have raised the bar for us mere mortals." She checked her messages again, she couldn't help it. The mundane details of her day job were topics she could deal with easily. "Anyway, I have a lot of time to figure out how to balance it all, and I should put in the hours whenever I can keep myself from vomiting or falling asleep."

"Nine months is not *that* much time if you think about it. Especially not when you have to move. You don't want to be packing up all those shoes when you're out to there."

Kate would have laughed again at his gesture of a large, third trimester stomach if she hadn't heard the rest of what he said. "Move?"

"Your apartment's hardly big enough." Adam put the magazine down and turned to her. "Maybe you won't even want to be in the city. It's tough to raise a kid here." As if he could sense the sudden chill she felt, he put his hand on her arm and squeezed gently. "We don't have to decide now," he said in a low voice. "Just something … we should … talk about."

It was so tempting to fall into a "we," to have a partner who could figure this out with her. It was such a false sense, though, Kate reminded herself. Their engagement was one of convenience. Their dating may have led somewhere, a real relationship maybe, if she could have learned to have one. "*I* can figure it out," Kate said steadily. "My job is in Manhattan, and I can't factor in a commute with my kind of hours." She lowered her voice and strained a smile, not wanting to garner pity from eavesdroppers who might think her baby had parents who disagreed on their basic life arrangements. "Plenty of people have babies in one-bedroom apartments. It's the New York way."

"You're not in this alone—you don't have to shut me out."

Kate shut her eyes, as if to close herself from the temptation of falling into him. She looked at him and whispered, "I won't hold you back."

"What? What you are talking about?" His eyes searched

hers, in honest confusion, Kate knew. She might hurt him a bit now, but she refused to hurt him more later on.

Her name was called by the nurse just then, and Kate gave a nod of thanks to the universe for sparing her from having a difficult conversation in absolutely the wrong place.

It was as if Adam was determined to play the role of excited first-time expectant father, despite how much Kate tried to spare him the responsibility. Once they were shown in to the examination room, he acted like their conversation had never happened, like they were any other couple, nervous with anticipation and endearingly awkward as she sat primly on the exam table in a paper gown.

"Where should I sit?" he asked, clearly never having accompanied anyone to a doctor's appointment before.

"Right in the chair next to me," Kate responded. "You're not ready for the stirrup view."

His eyes widened and he swallowed as he lowered himself into the chair Kate pointed at. "Probably not." He looked around at the artwork in the room and the posters illustrating the female anatomy, cracking his knuckles—a nervous tick Kate hadn't seen him do since they were in high school.

"Somehow your being nervous actually calms me down."

"I'm not nervous."

Kate leveled a look at him.

"OK, I am. Excited nervous, not scared nervous." He smiled at her and Kate could see that things would be OK. They could remain friends through all of this. An unconventional little family for this baby, but a loving one all the same. And without the expectations of a traditional family, she wouldn't need to worry about letting anyone down, not loving someone enough.

The doctor came in and greeted them then and proceeded to have Kate lie back for an ultrasound. One of the reasons Kate liked this doctor was because he was no-nonsense, cut through the chitchat, and she could be in and out of her appointments quickly. Kate swallowed any remaining nerves she might have had as Adam scooted closer to her and held her hand. It was nice to have someone to cling to, she had to admit, and while she couldn't expect him to accompany her on the myriad of appointments she'd have during this pregnancy, it was nice to have him here during the first one.

"It's supposed to look like a jelly bean," Adam whispered to her, as if sensing she was probably feeling a little unprepared for this appointment.

Kate smiled at him just as the doctor swung the monitor around for her to see the screen. "I'm afraid there is no fetus, Kate," he said. "I'm sorry." There was sympathy in his eyes, and his mouth curved into a small frown. Through the sudden haze she felt she wondered how many times he'd had to give news like this. She appreciated the sincerity in his tone, that he assumed this pregnancy had been planned, knew this baby was *wanted*.

He proceeded to deliver a string of sentences, with words that included, "chemical pregnancy … no gestational sac." But Kate barely registered the weight of what he was saying. It couldn't be. There had to be a mistake. This wasn't happening. She lay back against the cool pillow and stared at the ceiling.

They should really put artwork up there.

As the doctor removed his gloves and turned off the machines, she knew this moment was really happening.

"You mean, there was never a baby?" Adam asked. "Even though her bloodwork said she was pregnant?"

"It was technically a very early miscarriage—the body's way of ending an unhealthy pregnancy."

"So what now?" Kate asked, still staring at the blank white ceiling tiles. She should be relieved, shouldn't she? An unplanned baby that she no longer needed to plan for? Her friends would expect her to hardly miss a beat, to go back to the dirty-martini-drinking workaholic she'd always been. Isn't that what she herself expected? Yet all she felt was a palpable sadness, the likes of which she'd never felt before. For a baby she no longer had.

The doctor turned to speak to her. "You'll probably have some bleeding, then your body will go back to normal. You can even start trying again if you want to." He paused, as if to study her reaction. Kate schooled herself to have the best poker face of her life. "Take some time to grieve, Kate. If you need anything, my office can refer you to grief counseling—"

"That won't be necessary." Kate found her voice then. She would grieve just fine on her own. She moved to sit up and felt Adam's hand on her back. She wouldn't need his help anymore.

She couldn't really remember how she and Adam got back to her apartment, only that she'd somehow gotten dressed, that they gotten into a cab, and had barely spoken, barely even looked at each other.

"Are you … are you going back in to work today?" Adam finally asked, as he stood in her bedroom doorway.

Kate kicked her shoes off and sat on the edge of her bed. "Hardly any point now, I don't need that promotion so badly."

"Do you need to let anyone know you're out?"

Kate shrugged. In the cocoon of her own bedroom, she closed her eyes and placed a hand over her belly. The belly that would now stay perfectly toned and trim and stretchmark-free. Wasn't that what she'd strived for during all her workouts? She choked out a sob then, a noise completely unbidden, which took her by surprise. She opened her eyes to see Adam watching her and noticed now that his eyes were red-rimmed. The grief she saw in them undid her, and the sound that came from her own throat was almost unrecognizable even to her, a sound so awful in its sadness.

She cried into his chest, for how long, she didn't know. They said nothing, the only sounds coming from her sobs and his sniffles. She was grateful for his restraint, that he didn't break down in tears with her. It was selfish of her, she knew. He ought to be allowed to grieve for the baby that would have been both of theirs. But she needed him to be strong for the both of them at that moment, and he knew it. She held on to him a little longer, until finally she felt like she could breathe on her own, and pulled away to wipe her own tears.

She still couldn't bring herself to look at Adam again,

though, knowing she'd lose whatever composure she'd gained back once she saw the emotions in his face. "I was going to call him James," she whispered. "Ava if it was a girl." She didn't expect a response, but for some reason she felt the need to tell someone. She would have had a plan for this child by the time he or she was born.

"I know you wanted this baby," Adam said finally. "I know you loved it."

Kate could only nod, having no words to convey the relief she felt at having someone who understood what she felt at this moment. If someone had told her that she would feel this much pain over a baby that never was, she never would have believed them. She would have told them that her reaction would be relief … happiness, even, that she would be able to continue on with the life plan that *she* had control over. But Adam understood. He knew what a blessing this baby was to Kate, that she would have loved and cared for it in her own best way possible. She had understood that getting pregnant wasn't just about having a baby; it was about raising a small person, one who would have grown up in the heart of the greatest city on earth, one who she had already silently thanked for giving her the courage to stand up for herself at work, one who had helped her see that her life could be so much more than just about herself.

Chapter 27

The next day, Kate called in sick. Well, she emailed in to the boss's assistant that she was sick. And the next day she did the same, and the next and the next. The email went out at 5 a.m. every morning, just before Kate went out for her run, and she didn't check her messages at all. When her phone rang insistently with her office number on caller ID, she finally answered it. Her boss's assistant told her she'd missed a meeting with a major client and the boss wanted to know where she was. "Just tell him it's women's issues," Kate answered. "He'll stop asking you then." She hung up before any more questions could be asked.

It was only during her morning run that Kate felt any part of her former, regular self. And that was how she thought of herself now—pre-baby Kate and post-non-baby Kate. When her feet pounded rhythmically against the pavement and she breathed in the cold air indicating that fall was in full swing, she felt like she would recover from this grief she never thought she would feel. Adam stopped coming with her, thankfully, finally respecting her request to run alone. But when she got back to her apartment, he was almost always there, with his too-observant, too-caring gaze. How tempting it was to let him take care of her the way he promised, to let his cooking nourish her body, to let his love nourish her soul. But Kate didn't deserve him. It was her own tunnel vision of ambition and selfishness that kept getting in the way of letting him into her life before the baby and had prevented her pregnancy from developing normally. Oh yes, even though all the literature said that chemical pregnancies were unexplained, Kate felt in her heart that hers had everything to do with her age and tunnel vision focus on her career.

One morning after running ten miles of clarity, Kate returned with her plan. Adam would stay to care for her for as long as he thought she needed him. She had to release him, make him think her life was going back to normal, that she was over her grief, that he could move on to find someone else who was worthy of the love he had to offer, who could love him selflessly the way he deserved—and give him the family he wanted.

"No time for breakfast today," Kate said as cheerily as she could, as she practically bounced into her apartment and headed to her shower. "I'm going in to work—have a ton that's been piling up, I'm sure." *Careful.* This was the most she'd said to Adam in days. He might become suspicious.

After Kate got dressed in one of her best uniforms and did her hair and makeup, she exited her bedroom to find Adam leaning on the kitchen counter. "Listen, you've been so great, through this whole *thing*. I couldn't have gone through this without you." She couldn't bear to look at him and busied herself with shuffling things around in her purse. "I think it's time we both went back to our regular lives, don't you?"

Adam didn't say anything at first, just came around to face her. "If you need time to yourself, you only have to say so. I stuck around to make sure you were … OK. I mean, as OK as possible."

Ever the gentleman, ever the friend. "Well, I'm fine now. Thanks. I … ummm … think it's better if we spend some time apart."

Adam took her wrist to stop her movements. "Kate."

She looked up at him then and couldn't help but speak to him with the honesty she had with him in high school. To a point. "I need some time. I need to figure out how to move on without leaning on you. You need to move on. Fix your company, teach your class, meet some … other people." She felt the tears prick and refused to let them fall. "You can't be here all the time, taking care of me, waiting for me. It's like when we were in college—I need to figure this out on my own."

He let go of her wrist and sighed. "If that's really what you want, Kate."

"It is." She was relieved and sad at the same time. How Adam instilled such contradictory feelings within her, she couldn't imagine. "I'm grateful that we're friends, that we had some ... time ... together—"

"Grateful?" If it had been anyone by Adam, Kate would have felt like a complete idiot. But he just cocked a brow and pulled a half smile. "You're really bad at this breakup thing, aren't you?"

They both chuckled sadly. "You need to go back to California, Adam. Maybe not to Palo Alto, but back to the Bay Area where your friends are."

It was an easier goodbye when Kate knew she had to get to the office. She sat upright in a lounge chair outside her boss's door as his assistant arrived for the day. The older woman just shook her head at Kate and didn't say a word. Nor did her boss say a word or even look her way as he strode right by her on his way to his desk. Kate waited a few beats, heard him hang his coat and clear this throat, as if just wanting to make her squirm for a little longer. She wouldn't give him the satisfaction. She smiled at his assistant, who silently shook her head again.

"Get in here!" finally came the bellow.

Kate rose slowly, smoothed her skirt, and strode lightly into his office. Her boss stared at her from behind his desk, a vein bulging prominently from his forehead.

"I had some urgent medical problems that kept me out of the office."

Her boss stared.

"I'm fully recovered now, thank you for asking. But in light of recent events, I have decided to resign from my position here."

His eyes bulged and Kate swore she could see his pupils dilate. The door swung shut behind her, and Kate realized he'd pushed that infamous button on his desk that shut his office door, the button that she'd heard associates speak about but had never experienced for herself. She stood confidently, more sure of herself than she had been in a long time. "I'm prepared to give a few weeks' notice, to tie up any loose ends with clients so that they will still have a seamless, positive experience with the firm."

"You can't give notice."

"Excuse me?"

"You can't give notice when you're fired. And you'll leave here without any professional references. I'll tell your clients you've had a nervous breakdown. Or better yet, you left to become a *housewife*."

Kate was rendered speechless. Even she had underestimated her boss's outright lack of any professional demeanor. She smiled. "So does being fired mean I collect unemployment?"

"Get out."

"Wrongful termination. You should sue," Cass said over Starbucks. "I used to date a lawyer—trust me, you could win."

Kate texted Cass to meet her as soon as she turned in her security badge and clicked her stiletto heels out of the lobby for the last time. As expected, her friend was indignant over her "resignation." It felt good to have such close friends who always had her back, and even through her sadness, it felt right to have told Adam to go back to his. Kate shook her head. "I don't need those two more weeks of pay, I've got plenty saved up to carry me through until I figure things out."

"What *are* you going to do?" Cass softened.

"It's a little scary, I'll admit. I've *always* worked. Even through college I had multiple part-time jobs. I've never even taken more than a week off for vacation. Maybe I'll take one of those continuing education classes you're always raving about." Kate took the pins out of her hair and shook out her chignon. Her lipstick had long since come off on her coffee cup lid and she didn't bother to reapply. "One thing's for sure—I'm not going to tell Linda. She'll be hounding me day and night about it, spewing stats about how short term unemployment turns into long-term unemployment, yada yada yada."

"Does she know about … what happened?"

"That I was having a baby and then I wasn't, and that it's been the saddest experience that I don't think I'll recover from for a long time if ever?" It felt good to be able to half joke about it already, to know that Cass was a close enough friend that she wouldn't take Kate's words the wrong way. "It's a major turning point for me, maybe I'll tell her one day. Once I figure out *how* it's changed my life, not just that it did."

"You don't have to have everything in your life completely figured out before you let someone into it."

"Something tells me we aren't talking about my mother anymore."

"Your last texts to me were 'I sent Adam away' and 'I quit my job.' I'm just making sure you're not going completely off the deep end."

"You know I'm not good at this relationship thing. Adam deserves better than that. Than me."

"You just hadn't found the right guy yet."

"Is this where you try to convince me that Adam is The One?" Kate tried to joke. "Who are you, Suzanne?"

Cass paused and just stared at Kate for a moment. Then she smiled. "There's no convincing *you* of anything."

"What's that supposed to mean?"

Cass shrugged cryptically and raised her coffee in a toast. "Here's to your newfound free time … to do lots of thinking."

Kate walked home slowly, savoring the crisp fall air, thankful that she wasn't in a rush to get anywhere. What *would* she do with all her time? Catch up on her DVR? Take an exercise or yoga class that never seemed to fit into her schedule before? One thing she really didn't feel like doing was partying or socializing beyond her closest friends. She knew she needed time to herself, to process the loss of her would-be baby, to figure out how she was going to reprioritize her life.

Her apartment was quiet when she entered, eerily quiet and a little too dark now that Adam wasn't around. There was no trace of him, except for maybe the bowl of fruit on her counter that wouldn't have been there if she'd done the food shopping. She thought maybe he would have left her a note, but then again, they had already said their good-byes, hadn't they? She went to her bedroom to change into some jeans and a sweater, and that was when she saw it. Right on her pillow where she was sure to look. A Harlequin romance novel.

The couple on the cover looked much more updated than the ones she remembered from her youth. But there was no mistaking this was a story about a man and a woman finding true love. The kind of story she relished as a teenager and then somehow forgot about as she saw real-life love—and all its false starts and stops. Her favorite ones were when the main characters would resolutely deny their attraction to each other, only to find they were meant to be together after all. Her heart swelled involuntarily at the possibility that Adam was trying to win her back with this gesture.

Kate flipped through the book, hoping a note would drop out before she saw the inside front cover. "Hope you find your Happily Ever After. –A"

And with those six words, Kate knew he really was gone.

Just as she had asked.

Chapter 28

"Your friend moved out pretty quickly, yeah? Didn't have a lot of stuff, just like when he moved in." The front desk concierge in her building lobby handed Kate her dry cleaning—the last batch she would need to have done for a long while now that she didn't need to don her shark uniform. Normally she didn't mind the small talk, but did she need to be reminded of how quickly Adam left? That had been a week after they'd said good-bye, since she'd quit her job. Had he seized the freedom as soon as she offered it and taken the first flight back to California?

Another week had gone by, then another. She'd read the novel, plus a few more, watched two seasons of *How I Met Your Mother*, caught up on *Downton Abbey*, and tried three different exercise classes at the gym, including a spinning class that left her legs feeling like jelly for an entire day. She'd signed up for a cooking class—and then dropped it when she realized it was full of smug couples on the path to domestic bliss.

She had barely even seen the girls. She didn't know how to respond to their sympathetic gazes. It was even worse than when she fielded their concerned questions about her engagement to Alberto, which now seemed like a ridiculous lifetime ago. She didn't want them to worry about her. She had chosen this—she had chosen to quit, she had chosen to be alone while she figured out what was next for her. And yet her friends sensed that she didn't have that same confidence as she had when she so single-mindedly decided to take her career into her own control with her fake engagement.

And she couldn't admit out loud that she missed Adam. She'd taken to walking all over Manhattan, sometimes taking the subway a few stops and then just ... walking. Everything reminded her of him, even passing by places they'd never even been together. It was as if she was seeing the city through new eyes, through his eyes that wondered if New York was a good place to live. Would he really have left Palo Alto and moved here permanently to be with her and their baby? Would he have lived downtown? Or would he have wanted views overlooking Central Park in the super family-friendly Upper West Side? He would have lived downtown, of course, because that was where she and the baby would have been, and as responsible as he was, he would have chosen to be close by.

Now he was free to fall in love with some California girl and have babies with golden, sun-kissed hair. To live in an even more perfect version of the house she'd seen him with Claudia in.

Sometimes when she ran in the morning, she turned her music off to see if she could hear his footsteps behind her.

Now he could find someone who actually wanted a running partner.

It was during her morning runs when Kate realized how much she missed her work, too. Not the boss, obviously. She still felt remarkably free from being under his irrational scrutiny. But she missed her clients, she missed doing work for them, and she kind of missed her colleagues. too, and wondered if they could have been better acquainted if not for the boss's ways. Kate missed the work so much she even decided to volunteer her time at her local library branch, to do a seminar on how to take the first steps toward personal finance management. Maybe they were not the uber-wealthy clientele she had been used to, but it felt good to talk about how to gain financial freedom to those who really wanted it and needed it. And when she stayed an hour later than planned to answer questions, Kate felt like she'd made a difference to a few families at least, who maybe would have a few less arguments over where the paychecks were going.

During one of her long walks, Kate roamed the East Village, near her old stomping grounds at NYU, and then over to Cooper Union. She couldn't help going there, knowing he'd taught there. The whole city made her think of him anyway.

There were several groups of students milling around the sidewalk, laughing together, looking at each other's smartphones. Kate missed her student days in a way, when she felt so much excitement, so much possibility for an unknown future. Even as she'd told herself that the last several years had been filled with fun and unpredictable romantic adventures, this baby that wasn't was the first time in a long time that she had really looked *forward* to something, instead of focusing solely on the here and now.

It started to rain a little, big, fat droplets here and there, enough to send a few students scattering. Kate couldn't help but continue to watch them, to stand on this campus that wasn't hers. She hoped that the girl talking about stop motion video would go on to be a bigwig at some place like Viacom one day. Or the quiet one on the edges of her group would find her voice in a corporate boardroom. She could see how Adam had been inspired by teaching, being surrounded by so much natural, youthful energy. Would she have found the renewed energy in motherhood?

The rain started coming down harder, that bitterly cold fall rain that pelted through sweaters. Classes must have let out, as throngs of students began exiting the building and opening their umbrellas. Kate, of course, didn't have one of her own, so she took the mildly chaotic opportunity to duck into the building and out of the rain. She couldn't help roaming the halls a bit and was surprised when no one stopped her. She smiled to herself as she caught her reflection in a glass window display. Her damp hair fell across her shoulders, and her cheeks were pink from the chill. She certainly didn't pass for a student anymore, but she didn't look like she ought to be working in a corner office tower either. She peeked into emptying classrooms, wondering if Adam had taught in any of them.

And then in one of them, there was no mistaking the posture she'd come to know so well. His back was turned to her as he spoke with a student. His hands were in the pockets of his grey slacks and his shoulders strained against the blue button-down as if he couldn't wait to get out of his dress shirt. Kate felt a chill up her spine and leaned against the hallway wall, out of sight should Adam turn around. *He's still here.*

She ran her fingers through her hair and waited for the student to leave. She was surprised he was here, though she shouldn't have been, she realized now. Of course Adam would finish out the semester of teaching and stay for the duration of whatever commitment he'd made to the school. It was silly that she should feel her heart pounding so rapidly in her throat. On some level, she must have known she might run into him here, right? And she'd been practically looking for him everywhere she went in the city these days. During her runs, she thought about what she would say to him when she was ready—she'd been practicing.

The student left and Kate held her breath, willing herself to calm down. My goodness, this was just *Adam*. She closed her eyes and forced an image of high school Adam, bony and skinny, with glasses and crooked teeth, who carried exactly five blank sheets of loose-leaf paper every day because that was all he ever needed. She wouldn't feel nervous to talk to that guy. With her eyes still closed, she took a deep breath and turned through the doorway.

When she opened her eyes, she saw Adam perched on top of a desk, one ankle over his knee, flipping through a textbook. His pose was so much like the Adam she knew in school, and she realized she *was* nervous to talk to that geeky kid. She was in love with the best friend she had then, and she was in love with the man he'd become.

Adam looked up and any pleasure or shock at seeing her was quickly schooled behind an emotionless mask. She didn't blame him—she could be coming here to pick a fight with him for all he knew.

"Is there somewhere we can talk?" Kate managed to keep her voice normal, even though all she wanted to do was throw herself at him and ask him to forgive her for being so stupid.

Adam cleared his throat and crossed past her to shut the

door. "Nobody will bother us in here. I reserved the room for office hours." He pulled a chair out for her and then another one for himself to sit directly across from her. He smiled. "You look great. Relaxed."

"I've been great. It's been ... good ... for me, this break I'm taking."

He held her gaze as if looking to be sure she was telling the truth, and all Kate wanted was to lose herself in his blue eyes. How had she not seen how loving he was, how much she wanted to be a better person, a more caring person for him? How could she have kept pushing him away all this time? "You're staring at me like I have two heads," he smiled again.

"I'm staring at you like I'm seeing you for the first time." She longed to touch him, but didn't trust herself to get out anything she needed to say if she did. She reached out and touched his cuff, tracing her fingertip over the button. He didn't move, as if this was something they did every day.

"Do you like what you see?" He was trying to keep it light, to give her time to say whatever it was she'd come looking for him to say.

"I think we're worth a shot," she whispered. "More than a shot."

He took her fingers then, stilling them from the path along his cuff and brought them to his lips. "And?"

"I want to be with you. And only you. I haven't figured out everything ... anything ... about what my life is going to be like, but I want to see where it goes *with you*. I want you to stay here. In New York. For me." Kate started crying then—joy, relief, she wasn't sure which she felt more at finally having these words out loud, ones she'd been thinking even when she didn't want to admit them. "You're my best friend, you're... my partner ..."

Adam's eyes filled as he smiled and pulled her into his arms. "And?" he said cheerfully.

"And what? That's not enough?" Kate couldn't help but laugh as well, at this man who knew her better than anyone else, who gave her what she needed—time, space—and waited patiently for her to see for herself what he had known all along.

"And ...?" he smiled at her.

"You're great in bed." She smiled back at him. "Will you kiss me now, or do I have to do everything?"

And boy, did he kiss her.

When he finally stopped, when the room around her had stopped spinning, when she could open her eyes and finally, finally feel like she could see clearly for the first time in years, he stood her on her feet and stepped back. Without another word, he turned away from her to get something from his bag. When he turned back, he held out a ring that looked like the one she'd bought for herself from a street vendor, only this one sparkled like none she'd ever seen. And this one came in a box that said *Harry Winston*. Kate could do nothing but stare at Adam, at this man she thought she knew so well, but who could still surprise her beyond her wildest dreams. The man who fulfilled dreams she didn't know she had.

"This," he gestured around the room, "may not be the most scenic, picturesque place, and there aren't any flash mobs or singers involved, but Kate, you know I'm about more than the romance. I'm about more than a grand gesture." He got down on one knee then and looked up at her. "It has always been you, Kate. I love you. Will you marry me?"

Epilogue

Six Months Later

It was one of those spring days that had dawned chilly and brisk for Kate's morning run, but became that perfect blend of warmth and sunshine for her evening ceremony. Adam had won their debate about the venue—Kate couldn't imagine planning an outdoor wedding when there was no way she could control the weather. But she had to admit that the Pond at Central Park was perfect for their small gathering. And at least they had agreed upon that. Only closest friends and family were with them—Cass, Suzanne, and Mia sat in the front row next to Kate's parents. Adam's entire family, including all his brothers, their wives, and children took up nearly the entire groom's side in a rare show of support.

As she walked down the aisle, Kate exchanged a smile with Jane, who had quickly become a close friend, and the only person aside from Adam who knew her secret. It wasn't something she meant to keep from her girls very long, but after Kate had been caught sneaking off to the ladies' room one too many times, Jane had asked her point-blank if she was pregnant. Kate had been embarrassed to admit it at first, since she'd just started working for Jane three months ago and hadn't thought she'd get pregnant so quickly. But nothing could have dampened Kate's joy and relief after her first ultrasound showed a tiny little jelly bean of a baby with a strong heartbeat. Jane had been nothing but happy for Kate since she guessed her news, even going as far to say that mothers made some of the best employees since they knew how to multitask and use their time more efficiently than anyone else.

Kate tried to suppress her laughter as Adam took her hands, stared at her, at her stomach and then back up to her face. It was supposed to be a serious moment, wasn't it, as they prepared to say their "I Do's." But as if he could read her mind, they both broke into a laugh of pure joy and disbelief that they'd known each other for most of their lives and yet only just realized how much they completed one another.

Wendy Chen was born and raised in New York City and now lives in northern Virginia with her husband and kids. She is also the author of *Liar's Guide to True Love*. When she isn't working on her next novel, she can be found editing contemporary romances with Entangled Publishing. She has worked at *The Washington Post*, Random House, and iVillage. Connect with her on Twitter and Facebook where she muses about reading, writing, marketing, and motherhood.

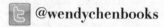 @wendychenbooks

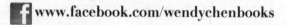 www.facebook.com/wendychenbooks